BIG MAN, BIG MOUNTAIN

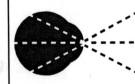

This Large Print Book carries the
Seal of Approval of N.A.V.H.

BIG MAN, BIG MOUNTAIN

WADE EVERETT

WHEELER PUBLISHING
A part of Gale, Cengage Learning

GALE
CENGAGE Learning·

Detroit • New York • San Francisco • New Haven, Conn • Waterville, Maine • London

GALE
CENGAGE Learning·

LIBRARY OF CONGRESS CATALOGING-IN-PUBLICATION DATA

Everett, Wade.
    Big man, big mountain / by Wade Everett.
        pages ; cm. — (Wheeler Publishing large print western)
    ISBN 978-1-4104-5575-8 (softcover) — ISBN 1-4104-5575-0 (softcover) 1.
    Large type books. I. Title.
    PS3553.O5547B543 2013
    813'.54—dc23   2012043025

Published in 2013 by arrangement with Golden West Literary Agency.

BIG MAN, BIG MOUNTAIN

1

Shaw Dance ate his supper while there was still some daylight left, and, after he'd washed the dishes and put his cabin in neat order, he picked up his .40-82 Winchester and went out to the front porch where he sat with it across his knees and watched the shadows grow long and deep. He lived in a high place, halfway up the face of a mountain that was far too rugged for any man to fully climb. Shaw Dance liked it that way, living alone, asking no man to do for him what he could not do for himself.

In years he was not old, barely thirty, but he had a quick and independent mind that had gathered a lot of knowledge and that always made a man appear older than he really was. In height he was an exact six feet, and he had long, powerful arms and a thick upper body but slim at the waist. His face was angular and rather set in features; he gave men the impression that he saw very little in life that was amusing.

Waiting did not try Shaw Dance's patience; he'd been waiting six nights in a row now and all that day the feeling had been strong that he wouldn't have to wait much longer.

A creek ran behind Shaw Dance's place, and farther up the mountain face there was a waterfall fed by a subterranean spring. Near this water source was Dance's mine, a shaft plunged deep into the mountain, and from this he took out what gold he needed and left the true richness of the vein untouched.

Dance knew how much gold was there, and the wind and the sky knew, and that was enough to suit him. He was not a man who shared a confidence with others.

The exact location of Shaw Dance's mine was no secret to the people of Summit, yet it was not a freely accessible place; the trail to it had been carved out of solid rock and there was barely room for a laden pack mule. Unfamiliarity with this trail had cost one man his life when he had tried to travel it at night, and without Dance's permission. Because of this, Dance took no special precautions in guarding it when he made infrequent trips into Summit, the town at the base of his mountain.

Yet the trail was not the only danger intruders faced. Two years before a man had tried to take a look at the mine, and Dance brought him down off the mountain in his wagon and the judge had decided that if a fellow didn't have any better sense than to poke around another's claim, he deserved to be shot!

Now Shaw Dance waited to shoot another, only this time it was different.

Frank Slate didn't want the gold. He didn't even want to look at the mine. Old Christian Slate, the father, had enough gold of his own to buy the mountain, and, as far as his four sons were concerned, he had been more than generous. The valley had belonged to Christian Slate for more years than people could remember, and it was a rich valley with Slate cattle everywhere, Slate riders patrolling it, and Slate money circulating in the town.

Frank Slate didn't have any business on the mountain. No real business. No, Dance decided, he just wants to come here and push me off my mountain. He's just a kid who sees another walking a fence and can't stand it, so he knocks him off.

Well you come on, Dance thought. You come on and push me off.

This was something he could understand,

this desire of Frank Slate, this desire to have because someone else had it. The Slates liked the valley; they had no use for the mountains. Dance guessed that Frank Slate just couldn't stand to see someone value a thing he had once thrown away.

And Dance knew that there wouldn't be any warning when Frank Slate showed up; the man knew enough of Indian ways, knew enough about Shaw Dance not to be that foolish. No, Dance decided, he'll come up wind quiet, with killing on his mind, and it won't be easy for me or him.

Dance ran his fingers over the cool receiver of the rifle and waited.

He wanted a smoke pretty badly; he always enjoyed a pipe after his evening meal and he missed it now, more because it was a break in his habits, which were long established.

He halfway wished there was a moon out so he could see a little, but, then, Frank Slate would be able to see too. One thing was as bad as another. The night was clear although no stars were visible. Dance could see the town of Summit, the streets clearly outlined by lamplight. Beyond, and farther down the valley, the lights of Christian Slate's ranch house were faint, yet distinct. And across the short stem of valley the dark

10

flanks of a line of mountains loomed blackly. Hidden by the timber was Max Bucher's sawyer camp, and during the day Dance could hear the steam donkey puffing away and the faint ring of the gang saw. Lower on the slopes, and barely a mile from town, the lights of the mine office gleamed clearly, and Dance wondered if Roe Carlyle was looking through his telescope now, waiting to see if he could catch a glimpse of gun-flash.

They all want my mountain, Shaw Dance thought. This amused him even as it annoyed him, for his mountain was not a beautiful thing, not symmetrical at all. The base extended broadly along the line of the valley. It was timbered thickly on the lower reaches, then grew to sheer rock bluffs on the top third. Once, Dance had seen it from a distance of forty miles and it had reminded him of a man's head with a lump protruding through the dark hair.

Ugly damned thing, Dance thought. No good to anyone but me, but they all want it.

He didn't know what time it was and didn't care particularly. He could sleep tomorrow, up there in the rocks where only the lizards and rattlesnakes moved.

Well, come on, Frank. It's harder just to sit here and wait than it is to fight you.

Shaw Dance listened to the slight night sounds, the faint whir of insects, the rasping sound of a buck down the canyon, scraping the moss off his horns. And Dance got to thinking that maybe he was out there now, hidden, waiting for him to make a move, just waiting for a sound to shoot at.

Very carefully he reached out and touched the latch string and pulled it, feeling the oak stick lift in the notch. Then he eased away and with the barrel of his rifle he pushed open the door, slowly, knowing that the old iron hinges were going to squeak.

It sounded like the caw of a sick crow, and from out in the black yard, low to the ground, a shotgun boomed and a load of buckshot slammed into the door, flinging it wide open.

Dance dropped the hammer on his rifle and before the echo of the shot died away he had flung himself off the porch. Barely in time too, for Frank Slate used the other barrel of his shotgun, peppering the spot Shaw Dance had vacated. Dance felt two of the thirty-two caliber pellets bite into him, one in the flesh part of his arm and the other low on the side, and he thought, a man can't come much closer to dying.

He stood straight, hipped his rifle, and emptied the magazine in a spatter of bullets wide enough to take in any roll that Slate might make in either direction. He heard the man grunt, and Dance crouched down behind the edge of the porch and loaded the Winchester.

Frank Slate broke open the shotgun; Dance could hear the mechanism cock itself, and he waited to hear it snap shut.

In a moment, he heard it.

And he heard Frank Slate speak. "Dance?" The voice was full of pain — strained and hardly recognizable.

Dance smiled, and thought, "Want me to say something, don't you? Want me to give you a target for those two barrels."

He let many minutes pass in stone silence, then Slate said, "Dance, help me! I'm gut shot!"

All right, Dance thought. I'll help you. He moved soundlessly until he was protected by the long wall of his house. Cupping his hands around his mouth to throw the sound against the backdrop of rock, he said, "You're lying to me, Frank."

He knew how this would sound to a man in the yard, as though he had slipped away from the cabin and made it to the brush skirting his yard. The last syllable of his words was drowned completely by the roar of Slate's shotgun, and Dance heard the

13

twin charge rip into the brush. He jumped clear of the wall and pumped the magazine empty, and this time Slate screamed and started to thrash around on the ground.

No pretending this time, Shaw Dance knew, and reloaded his rifle, taking his time about it. The shotgun pellets in his arm and side were beginning to hurt, and he was bleeding freely; his hand was sticky and he could feel the blood soaking his underwear at the belt line.

Frank Slate was moaning and kicking and bubbling through his nose and Dance knew that he'd gotten a lung, probably a ranging shot that reached down into the vital abdominal organs. He didn't like the taste this left in his mouth, but he would have to finish this. He walked across the dark yard and nearly stumbled over Frank Slate. Dance kicked the shotgun away and went on back to the cabin for a lantern. He lit the inside lamps and the lantern and returned to the yard, casting a round puddle of yellow light ahead of him.

Slate was on his belly, face down in the dirt, and the .40-82 had gone clean through him. Dance rolled him over and Slate looked at him, his eyes wide and covered with a slick film. "God damn — you," he gasped.

There was no sympathy in Shaw Dance's voice. "What the hell did you do it for, Frank?"

"No man's got — a right — to a whole — mount — in." He stared and died and went on staring, his expression fixed forever in surprise and pain and disappointment.

Shaw Dance continued to look at the dead man, gone now at twenty-six, thrown away, a victim of his stubbornness, his foolishness. "What a waste," Dance said and went into his cabin. He placed the rifle by the door and stripped to the waist and stood before the mirror to see how badly he was hurt. The pellets were still in him; he knew he'd have to go to Summit to the doctor or get lead poisoning.

He bandaged his arm with a clean piece of cloth, and made a compress for his side, winding the bandage tightly around his waist. Then he put on another shirt, picked up his rifle, and went outside.

He wheeled his buckboard from the lean-to barn, hitched up the team, then got a blanket to wrap Frank Slate in. Loading the man was a chore, but he managed it. Then he put his rifle against the seat and got in, taking the road down the mountain. It wasn't much of a road; rather it followed the natural slashes and draws, and his only

15

improvement had been to hoist the biggest boulders out of the way. At the timbered stretches the road was smoother, with a semblance of order, and it was here that he found Frank Slate's horse.

Dance stopped, tied the horse on behind, and drove on again.

It took him forty minutes to reach Summit, and, if he could have made it in quicker time, he wouldn't have for he didn't like the town, or any town; a man had to watch himself all the time in those places for trouble lurked around every corner. Yet he guessed it wasn't the towns, just the people. You put a lot of people together and you get hate and greed and prejudice and a lot of evil foolishness.

Summit wasn't much to start with, just a main street with a few more running crossways to it, and the alleys behind. The residences were crowded against the surrounding hillside like bugs clinging to the bark of a tree. The whole town was built on a slant; the main street had a sharp tilt to it, and the cross streets were steep enough to make a man puff. The houses went up in tiers with the families at the highest able to gawk down on their neighbors below.

Still the town was prosperous; it was supported by three factions, each trying to out-money the other. Christian Slate's cattle empire had built the town, but in late years mining had added a great deal in wealth, and even Max Bucher with his saw camp was swelling the community fortune.

Dance was somewhat flattered that they looked to his mountain with envy, because it was a tall mountain all right, and because he supposed there weren't many men who owned a mountain all to themselves, owned it legal and clear. Christian Slate wanted it because it would make a good monument to his valley empire. Max Bucher wanted it because there was timber on it, and he didn't have the nerve to cut a stick of it as long as Shaw Dance sat up there and looked down like an angry god. And Roe Carlyle, too. He wanted the mountain because there was some gold in it, and it would impress his company if he could get control of it.

As he reached the end of the main street and saw the people there, Dance knew that they were waiting to see who was coming down the mountain. The moment they saw his buckboard, a kind of sigh moved up and down the street, like a paper pushed along by the wind, and he couldn't make up his mind whether they regretted the outcome, or were glad. He drove past them, hardly glancing their way, yet seeing them all, every detail of their curious faces and mouths chewing on tobacco or cigars.

And he saw the fancy buggy belonging to Christian Slate tied in front of the hotel, flanked by the tied horses of his three remaining boys, Morey, Kyle, and Leed. The silver on their saddles caught and reflected the lamplight as he passed on.

Dance drove to the sheriff's office and stopped there but didn't get down. Behind him, in the street, the crowd moved forward from both sidewalks. The door of the sheriff's office opened and Cove Butler stepped out. He was a slender, dry-mannered man with a bland face that masked a dangerous mind. "I see Frank didn't make it," Butler remarked and lifted a corner of the canvas to see where Slate had been hit; he had that kind of a curiosity.

Through the crowd, the bulk of Christian Slate moved like a giant wave before the blunt bow of a sailing vessel. Shaw Dance turned in his seat and picked up his rifle, letting his broad thumb rest on the hammer; the muzzle was casually pointed in the direction of Christian Slate, not at him, but near enough so that it wouldn't be any trouble to bring it to bear if he had to.

Cove Butler said, "You won't need that, Shaw."

"How can you tell?" Dance asked.

Christian stopped as though he had run aground on a shoal. "Is that my boy there?" He pointed to the canvas-covered body. His sons came through the crowd and lined up alongside of him as though to present a united front; they had to elbow people aside to do it, but they were Slates and sure that no one really minded too much.

"I'm going over to the doc's," Shaw Dance said, speaking to Cove Butler. "You want to lift him out?"

"You didn't answer me!" Christian Slate bellowed.

"Do I have to?" Dance asked. A part of the crowd eased around to the front of his team, yet he felt no threat from them. Christian Slate stood there a moment, then nodded his head and two of his boys lifted Frank from the back of the buckboard and laid him on the wooden walk.

Without waiting any further, Shaw Dance drove on, letting the motion of his team part the crowd. He passed through without brushing any of them. He could hear Christian Slate's anguished shouting, and Cove Butler's strong, authoritative voice, then he turned the corner and put this behind him.

Tying his team, he went up the walk and knocked on the door, and a woman in the

19

parlor put down her magazine and came to answer it. She looked at him and said, "Come in, Shaw. I've been expecting someone, either of you, although I was sure it would be you."

He smiled at her and in the hall light his face was pleasantly angular, tight of flesh, with a good bone structure. His hair was more red than brown, and his mustache was thick, carefully trimmed.

Dance said, "I won't have to take my pants down this time, Jane."

"The shyness of men is a genuine paradox," Jane Meer said. "Come on in the office and sit down." She saw the blood soaking through his shirt. "I knew one of you would be hurt — the other dead."

He went with her to the back room and sat on the operating table while she adjusted the wick of the lamp with a reflector on it. Without being told, he took off his shirt and dropped his underwear around his waist. He seemed a little embarrassed when she put a hand on his bare chest and gestured him to lie flat. Then she examined the wounds, probed them with a fine wire, and found the pellets.

"Buckshot?" she asked. "What did you use?"

"A rifle."

She was a small woman in her late twenties, very business like. Her hair was light and would have bleached to a nice blonde if she'd got out in the sun a little more. Her face was round and very attractive, and even the glasses she wore did not distract from her appearance. She probably hurt her eyes reading all those books to become a doctor: this was Dance's thought as she boiled her instruments.

She was gentle, sure of herself, and she worked fast so that the pain he endured was brief. Yet through the hurt of it all he was conscious of her soft hands, as though his mind was working on two planes at once.

When she dropped the pellets in the pan, she said, "Did you have to kill him?"

He thought a moment. "You don't stop a man like Frank Slate without killing him. Besides, he put those two pellets into me before I hit him."

She put her hands on his chest and looked at him over the tops of her glasses; they had a habit of slipping part way down her nose when she worked and she had the habit of always reaching up and pushing them back in place. "Why did he really come up the mountain, Shaw?"

"Before he died, he said that no man had a right to a whole mountain. He just saw something that he wanted. No one made him come up there, Jane. Last week he made his brag, and something inside him just drove him, I guess."

"Are you sure you never made him come up?"

"I don't understand."

"I have two brothers, both successful. One is an attorney and the other is a publisher of a big newspaper in Chicago. My father was disappointed because I was a girl; he always wanted a third son to be a doctor. And because he wanted that, because he made me feel at fault, I became a doctor. He was never happy about it."

Shaw Dance said, "I've never baited Frank Slate."

"No, but you want something, Shaw, and it bothered him." She turned and started to bandage his arm. "Maybe I don't know the why of it, but you've always seemed to be a man who wanted revenge, yet hadn't quite made up his mind just what form it would take."

Someone opened the outer door and came down the hall and knocked. "Jane? It's Cove Butler. Can I come in?"

"The door's unlocked," Jane Meer said and went on with the dressing.

Butler came in and closed the door and

stood by Shaw Dance. The lamplight cast blues and pinks into the pearl handled pistol he wore. He looked at Shaw Dance and said, "Scattergun? I won't insult you by asking whether or not it was a fair fight."

"I waited for him on the porch," Dance said. "That's all the advantage I'll give any man."

Butler sighed. "Well, I don't suppose there's a man in Summit who didn't hear Frank Slate brag that when the sun came up one of these days he'd be sitting on your porch watching it." He brushed a hand across his smooth cheek and flounced his mustache once or twice. "It makes a man wonder what the fool was thinking of."

"I guess he just wanted to look out a far piece. He wouldn't be the first man who wanted another man's view."

"That's as good as any," Butler said. "The old man's taking the body home for burial. It makes a man think. The mother and the sister sit home and have dead kin brought to the door. It's no wonder women take to four walls and never care if they leave the house." He glanced at Jane Meer. "Is he going to be all right?"

"He's not going to feel like doing a jig," she said. "Why?"

Butler clung to a momentary silence.

"Because Morey Slate and his two brothers haven't left town yet." He gave Dance a pat on the shoulder. "I'll wait for you outside."

After Butler closed the door, Jane Meer said, "You've killed two men over that mountain. When will it stop, Shaw?"

"When people stop wanting what ain't theirs." He sat up, tried his arm and found that it worked. "When Christian Slate first came to this valley as a young man, he just looked around and said, 'This is mine.' From time to time he's backed up his right to it, and now he has clear title. I'm the same way, Jane. Born with nothing, and for the first twenty years of my life it seemed that nothing was all I'd get. And all the time I kept looking at that ugly mountain and wondered why I shouldn't go up there and look it over. So I climbed it, and like Christian Slate, I'll stay there."

She tidied up, putting away her instruments, and hanging a towel up to dry. "The higher you climb, the lonelier it gets, Shaw. I fought to be a doctor. Fought my parents, the teachers, and I've fought other doctors. Now I'm a doctor, but I'll never be able to make people believe it. Four-fifths of the population of this town will ride forty miles to Quartzsite to see the doctor there, because he's a man."

"They're all fools."

"Are they? Maybe we're the fools, Shaw. You for refusing to give up that mountain. Me for refusing to admit that a doctor has to be a man. I'm not a bad looking woman, Shaw, but men don't propose to me."

He shrugged. "Someday I'll give up and be the old man of the mountain and you'll be an old maid. Why cry about it? We picked the road we travel; so we've got no kick coming when we stub our toes."

She helped him on with his shirt and buttoned it for him. "When you get to the top of that mountain, you'll just have to come down. No place else to go."

"We're not going to get anywhere with this kind of talk," he said, reaching into his pocket for his purse. "How much for digging the lead out?"

"Six dollars." She took the money and held it in her hand. "You'd better come back in three days and let me have another look. I'll want to change the bandages then too."

"All right," he said and turned to the door. But he stopped there. "Jane, you're right about one thing: you ain't a bad looking woman. And I just don't think of you as a doctor at all."

He didn't stay to study her reaction, or to hear what she might have to say about it; he closed the door, walked through her house, and stepped outside. Cove Butler was standing by the stone hitching post.

Butler said, "You've got your rifle; good. I'll buy you a drink, Shaw."

"Is that where they're waiting? In Hanley's saloon?"

"It's a Slate hangout," Butler said. "Christian Slate and his sons have bought a drink for every plank in the place." He walked along with Shaw Dance and now and then shot him a sidelong glance. "I'll back you if there's any trouble tonight."

"Better not take sides," Shaw Dance advised.

"I take the law's side," Butler said flatly. "I'd turn on you in a second if you broke the law, Shaw."

"Fair enough," Dance said and fell silent.

Hanley was doing a good business because the three Slate brothers were standing at his bar, bringing with them the wild independence of rich cattlemen that always promised trouble. And there was nothing that could draw business like trouble.

Butler went in first and stopped just inside, so close to the door that Shaw Dance had to step around him. Everyone turned their heads except the Slate boys; they stood there, shoulders hunched, looking into the back bar mirror.

When Dance approached the bar, men moved aside to make a place for him, but he indicated that he wanted to stand next to Morey Slate. He laid his rifle flat on the bar, the muzzle of it pointing down the bar where the Slates stood. Dance said, "Whatever they're having." Then he looked at Morey Slate. "The next time I come to town I'll bring Frank's shotgun with me."

There was no sound in the room save the rap of the bottle neck against the glass rim, and when the bartender placed the drink in front of Shaw Dance, he spilled some of it.

Morey Slate said, "It might be just as convenient if one of us came up there after it." He looked at Dance, his grey eyes flat and steady. Morey was a good looking man in his middle thirties, and he had a reputation with women that wasn't confined to Summit. He was tall and slender and cut a fine figure on the dance floor, and there was a latent danger in the man that attracted women. Then too, he was a Slate, which made him a big man without half trying.

"You're welcome to do that," Dance said evenly. "Let me know when you're coming and I'll have coffee on. But I'd come in the daylight. The pass can be dangerous at night."

Morey stared a moment, then turned to his drink and tossed it down. He said, "Frank threw himself away on a fool brag. I'm smarter than that."

"Yes, and you'll live longer that way." Dance leaned his arms on the bar. "With a whole valley to ride around in, a man would think you'd be too tired to climb the mountain."

"One of these days you're going to come down like a rolling rock," Morey said. "And I'd like to give you the shove that starts you off."

"What's up there that you want so bad, Morey? Not the gold."

"You're up there," Slate said. "I just don't like the thought of a man sitting up there and looking down on me. Especially a man I've never liked. I used to beat you once a month when I was a kid, but you'd never say calf rope for me. We Slates don't like a proud man, Dance. Especially one who ain't got any reason to be proud."

"I don't bother you," Dance said softly. "I've never bothered the Slates. You, Frank, and Kyle, you've always brought the fights to me."

"But you bother me," Morey said. "You bother me when I walk into Reilly's store and see you standing there and you look at

28

me as if I wasn't there at all. You bother me now, standing there, looking down on me like you were still up there on the mountain. You've got to go, Shaw. You've just got to. I knew that when you were ten years old."

"Morey, you've always made this up in your own mind. I leave you people alone, and I always have." He twirled his whiskey glass and left wet rings on the bar. "I defend what's mine, Morey, just as you'd defend what's yours. So stay away from my mountain. I don't want to kill another of you."

"I ain't going to talk any more about it," Morey said and nudged his brothers. They all stepped away from the bar, Morey first because he was the oldest, then Kyle, and then Leed, who was barely twenty, but as wild as any two of them combined. He was a small man, smaller than Christian Slate liked a son to be, but he made up for it in pure meanness. Leed's face was thin and dark, and like most small men, he wore the biggest pistols he could buy, .44 Remingtons with eight inch barrels.

As Leed passed Shaw Dance, he asked, "How come you never fought me, Dance?"

The others stopped and Morey frowned. Shaw Dance said, "Because you were such a little squirt that I didn't want to hurt you."

Dance knew, in round terms, what this

would produce, and he grabbed Leed by the neckerchief and pulled him toward him even as he swung the rifle and jammed the muzzle hard against the young man's chest. Leed's hands were on his pistols, but he didn't draw them. Dance said, "Now if I pulled this trigger, I'd powder burn a hole clean through you, sonny. That would be kind of messy in Reilly's sawdust, wouldn't it?" He stared into Leed's round, surprised eyes and waited.

Morey Slate said, "Let him go, Dance. You don't want to kill him."

"The question is, does he want to kill me?" He let go of Leed's neckerchief and reached down for the portside pistol, lifted it from the holster and placed it on the bar. He then relieved Leed of the other gun.

Morey said, "Come on, you've got another pair at home."

"I want those back," Leed said. He was at that age where he lacked the sense to make a good judgment, yet was stubborn about the one he did make.

"We'll get 'em back," Morey said. He took Leed by the arm and towed him out of Reilly's saloon.

After they left, Cove Butler drew a long breath and everyone seemed to talk at once. Butler said, "I haven't bought you that drink yet, Shaw." He wiggled his finger at the bartender, who was busy now, topping glasses. Outside, the Slates mounted their horses and rode out of town, and then Butler relaxed even more. He said, "Are you going back tonight?" Dance nodded. "Better watch the road then."

"They won't bushwhack me on the road," Dance said evenly. "Leed might think about it, but he's afraid of what Morey or his father would do if he carried it through."

"I wouldn't bet on that."

Dance shook his head. "You heard Morey. Killing me here wouldn't mean a thing. That's why nothing happened tonight." He pointed up. "They want me to come down like a rolling rock. Remember?"

"I still don't know why," Butler said.

"Just to be doing it," Dance said. "What makes one dog bite another?"

2

Roe Carlyle was in his office at the smelter when he got the news. One of his men came in without knocking and Carlyle looked up. A shaded desk lamp concentrated the light on his paperwork and the upper part of his body was in darkness.

"Well," Carlyle asked, "who came back?"

"Dance," the man said. He stood there in the doorway as though he didn't want to come in, but just to be excused so that he could get back to town.

Carlyle threw his pencil down and swore. "He has the devil's own luck, hasn't he?"

"He shoots fair to middlin' too," the man said.

"Where is Dance now?"

"Over to Doc Meer's gettin' some buck-shot picked out of him."

Carlyle chuckled. "That close, huh? All right, Fred, you go and tell Hanley that I said to give you a drink on my account."

After the man left, Roe Carlyle raised the shaded lamp and walked over to another desk and took a bottle from the drawer. He could have offered the man a drink from it, but he felt that to do so would breed a familiarity that he didn't want. It was a chore requiring constant attention, this keeping the common man in his place.

Carlyle had his drink and put the bottle away. He was not a big man, but he was substantial enough, with a good, thick chest and an aura of power about him. He was an educated man and very proud of it, and he attributed his position as chief executive to this, and his natural ability to handle men.

Which wasn't bad for a man in his mid-thirties.

If Shaw Dance was at Doctor Meer's place, Roe Carlyle figured that he had time enough to get to town before he left. He didn't think it would hurt to talk to Dance again; the man might be getting tired of people bothering him and be more reasonable toward an offer to buy the mineral rights to the mountain.

Carlyle locked his office because he believed that all his subordinates snooped when he was gone, and got a horse from the company stable. He waited while this was saddled for him, then rode toward Summit. Although there was no moon, Carlyle could see the mountain looking up like some slumbering giant, a dark pinnacle against a dark sky, and in his mind's eye, Carlyle could see every crag, every sawtooth ridge, for he had been studying that mountain in detail for some years. Almost every day he would sit in his office window with his telescope and look at the mountain, like a man will study a thing that is not yet his, but which he knows will someday be his.

By the time he got to town, the crowd had already formed in Hanley's, and because he disliked crowds, Carlyle went over to the hotel porch across the street and sat; the view was good and he was satisfied to be an onlooker.

He took a chair and propped it against the wall and lit a cigar. A few minutes later Roan Gentry came out. He was a withered old man with a bad hip and a bad disposition and the hotel was his, a fact that he allowed few people to forget.

"He ain't dead yet," Roan Gentry said and sat down.

"I know that," Carlyle said with some irritation. He disliked this old man; he disliked anyone who owed his good fortune to getting there first.

"But you're sittin' there wishin'," Gentry pointed out.

"If you want me to move from your damned porch," Carlyle said, "I'll do so."

"You might as well stay," Roan Gentry said. He fired up his evil smelling pipe and let the smoke drift across Carlyle's face. "When you goin' to take a trip up the mountain?"

"Why should I do that? I know what's up there."

"I'll bet you do," Gentry said. "You've been lookin' through that spy glass for some time now. Like a man peekin' through the crack in a shade of a sportin' gal's bedroom." He chuckled. "When you go up there, let me know. I'll bet five to three that you don't make it through the pass, and bury you fancy with the winnin's."

"You wouldn't bet on anything that wasn't a sure thing."

"My point exactly," Gentry said and puffed his pipe. "Still, a man can't help but wonder how much gold is up there. I wonder myself, now and then. I guess everybody does. But I never had the gold fever like some people. When I first saw this valley and looked at them mountains you could see where the ice a million years ago had clawed and shoved, pushin' up the rich ore into the flanks. The gold's on your side, Roe. The real gold anyway. But there's some on Dance's mountain, like the good Lord put it there just as a favor." He looked at Carlyle. "You know how to grade ore. What would you say he's got up there?"

"High grade," Carlyle said. "He never brings much down at a time, but I know it's high grade." He sighed and shied his cigar into the street. "But I don't think he's touched the good vein. It's higher. He hasn't reached it. Maybe he never will."

The Slate boys came out of Hanley's place and mounted up, tearing out of town immediately. Roe Carlyle turned his head and watched them go.

Gentry said, "Young Leed wasn't carryin' his guns. That's odd. He ain't much without 'em and I guess he knows it."

"Frank was a damned fool," Carlyle said. "They're all damned fools, the Slates. You don't tell a man you're after him, then go and get him."

"What do you tell him?"

"Nothing," Carlyle said. "Least of all, Shaw Dance."

Roan Gentry laughed. "The mountains have been here a long time, Roe. Funny only Dance ever took the notion to climb that one. I recall him as a kid, always lookin' at that mountain. Other kids looked at candy and some liked the fancy doodads over at the saddle shop, but Dance liked that mountain." He waved his hands at the black hills behind the town. "You fellas find the gold with book learnin', but there's others that know where the gold is. Dance knew, but he never went into them mountains. No, when he climbed that ugly hunk of rock it wasn't gold he was after. Gold is for little men, Roe, men with our greeds. Men like you and me."

"You're getting senile," Carlyle said, then stopped talking.

Shaw Dance and Cove Butler came out of Hanley's place. They paused for a moment, talking softly, then Butler started to walk on down the street.

Carlyle left his place on the porch and started across. Dance saw him and waited, the rifle tucked in the crook of his arm. As Carlyle came up, Dance said, "No, I haven't changed my mind."

"Hell, I haven't said anything yet," Carlyle protested.

"Well, you always say the same thing. The answer is no, I don't want to sell or lease."

"There's no reason for you to be so stubborn," Carlyle said. "I told you I'd go fifty thousand, finance the road building and all development. In ten years, the rights revert back to you."

Shaw Dance shook his head. "Roe, if I had fifty thousand dollars, what would I do with it?"

"Why, go someplace else, I guess."

"What for?"

This was a frustrating line of talk for Carlyle; it irritated him. "Damn it, people who have money travel!"

Dance smiled. "Roe, I can see for miles without taking a step. You're wasting your time."

"Maybe, but you had a close one tonight. Maybe the next time. . . ."

"Well then you ought to wait a little

37

longer," Dance suggested. He started to step past Carlyle, and the man took Dance by the arm, unthinkingly applying pressure to the wound. The sudden shoot of pain made Dance react instinctively; he clipped Carlyle in the pit of the stomach with the rifle butt and knocked him into the dust.

Carlyle acted as though he were going to vomit, and he held his hand tight to his stomach while the other braced him in a sitting position. He looked at Shaw Dance and said, "You shouldn't have done that. You're not so good a man can't touch you."

"Don't grab at me," Dance said. "I've never liked it."

Cove Butler hurried back down the street. He stopped and looked at Carlyle, then said, "What's the trouble here?"

"No trouble," Roe Carlyle said, getting up. His breathing was still painful, but he put on a good front and walked away, his step a bit unsteady.

Cove Butler asked, "What did you hit him for?"

"He grabbed my bad arm," Dance said. "I didn't think."

"Well, hell, why didn't you tell him that?" He could see that Dance hadn't; he knew without asking that he hadn't. "It wouldn't have hurt you any to have said something.

Shaw, if they don't understand you, it ain't always their fault."

"What difference does it make who's at fault?" Dance asked. "When I'm right, no one remembers. When I'm wrong, no one forgets."

"That's the philosophy of a man alone," Butler said. "And of a man who hates people."

"I like people to mind their own business and leave me alone," Shaw Dance said. "And that's why I'm now going home. So I won't be bothered."

"I was going to ask you to come home with me and have a cup of coffee." He took out his watch and looked at it. "At two o'clock, my wife always puts a pot on. Will you?"

Dance hesitated, then nodded and walked with Butler to a side street, then hiked up the hill with him. They went in the front door and Butler took off his gunbelt and hung it on the halltree. Dance leaned his rifle against the wall and followed him into the kitchen where Butler's wife was making coffee.

She was a plump, moon-faced woman with a buxom figure swathed in a woolly robe. Butler kissed her briefly, inquired as to the children's behavior, then sat down at the table, and motioned for Dance to do the same.

"I've made some sandwiches," Clara Butler said. "Cold ham. You're hungry enough to eat one, aren't you, Shaw?"

"I'll eat anything that isn't my own cooking," Dance said and smiled.

After setting out the sandwiches and coffee, Butler's wife joined them and Dance remained clear of the conversation, unless drawn into it. He knew Butler, yet really did not know him at all, for the things he knew were of no real importance when judging the man and what he stood for. Butler was the first peace officer who had ever offered justice to the county. He was without fear, yet he maintained a delicate balance of mind where right and wrong were concerned.

Not wishing to intrude longer than necessary, Dance excused himself, saying that he had to start back.

"I left your team and rig behind the jail," Butler said. "Watch yourself on the road. It won't cost anything."

"All right," Dance said and left the house.

He found his buckboard and got in it and drove out of Summit. His side and arm pained in a throbbing manner, and he knew he wouldn't get any sleep that night. Tomor-

40

row it would be worse; he knew what it was like for he'd been hit once before, in the fleshy part of the leg.

He managed to put the team away and fill the grain box, then he went into his cabin, bolted the door, and tugged off his boots. Then he thought about it and got up and unbolted the door; he might have to go outside before morning and be too sick to fool with the bolt.

Supine on his bunk, the pain seemed more intense, and he figured by morning he would have a fever.

Dawn found him sick at the stomach and he crawled outside until this passed, then went back to bed. He slept part of the day, but it was a delirious rest, full of dreams of latent dangers, and he could not separate reality from fancy and he fired his rifle at all those people coming up the pass, and, when the Winchester was empty, he threw it away and systematically began to smash the things inside the cabin.

He fell exhausted on the floor.

When he woke, it was daylight, and he was in his bunk. He looked around and found a pile of broken dishes neatly swept into the center of the floor. His rifle was leaning by the door and he heard someone outside chopping wood.

Then Jane Meer came into the cabin and dumped wood in the box by the stove. She looked at him and said, "You've had a busy time of it." She made a fire and began to fix a meal.

She checked his temperature and found it going down, then finished cleaning up the place. Later she propped him up in bed and made him eat, and to his surprise the food stayed down. He felt that there was no reason for her to stay longer; she had already remained too long and people would talk about her. Still, he didn't think there was enough daylight left for her to make it off the mountain and the trail was too dangerous for her to attempt it at night.

Yet it bothered him for there were people in Summit who wouldn't believe that. They'd believe she had stayed because she wanted a man. They'd say that it was just the thing you'd have to expect from a woman who didn't have the decency to blush when a man took off his shirt.

They wouldn't all say that, but most of them would because they resented her and were suspicious of her and had already accused her of untrue things, all behind her back. Dance figured it was because she was a doctor, and a good one, and it made liars out of all those people who said it wasn't possible for a woman to be a good doctor.

He knew she had taken a lot of fresh lip off miners and cowboys and lumberjacks; they'd come to her pretending pain just to get smart with her, and afterward he bet she cried about it and cursed the chance that made her a woman.

He knew she never cursed the fact that she was a doctor.

That evening, he asked her, "Jane, do you hate people?"

"I hate some individuals," she said. "You?"

"I think I hate society," he said softly. "I like most people though." He rubbed his sprouting whiskers. "You're the first woman who's ever stepped into my house. I would have invited you before, but I didn't think it was a smart thing to do."

"People talk no matter what," Jane Meer said. "I'm used to it."

Dance shook his head. "You never get used to it. I know because I never did. My ma and pa were never married. I guess they meant to be but the country was wild and the nearest preacher was eighty miles across the mountains, so they just wrote their promise in the Bible and let it go at that. Summit wasn't much in those days, just Roan Gentry's store and saloon and a few other places, and most of the people here

43

understood that eighty miles was a far piece and a person could just go on putting off a thing." He shrugged. "Folks don't think anything of it if a man beds up with an Indian or a nigger, but when whites —"

"You think about it a lot, don't you?"

"It doesn't bother me anymore," he said and lowered himself to a flat position. "Christian Slate was pretty well fixed for money when he married his woman. My pa never had nothing to speak of. So Slate takes his woman eighty miles and married her, and ten years later his kids call me a bastard. No, it doesn't bother me now, but I still think about it when I see a Slate."

She came over to the bed and looked at him. "Shaw, I want an honest answer. Did you think of that when you killed Frank?"

"No," he said. "I only thought that it was a shame to waste a man that way."

His answer satisfied her, and she let him sleep.

Roe Carlyle stayed in his office until nine, then he turned out the lamp and stood at the window awhile, looking at the dark loom of the mountain. The night was clear and the air fresh, and, because he had nothing else to do, he got out his telescope, mounted it on the stand, and stood there with his eye to it. The instrument was powerful, with a finely ground set of lenses from Germany, and he focused it carefully on Shaw Dance's place. A pinpoint of light caught his attention, and he concentrated on it, hoping that it was a fire. It would have pleased him to see Dance's place burn to the ground.

The light grew stronger, then he realized that someone had lit the lamp and put the chimney in place. He thought about this and wondered whether Dance had lit it, or Jane Meer. He knew she was up there for he had seen her leave town, and the hostler at the stable had told him her destination.

Which made Carlyle wonder if Dance was more seriously injured than he had realized. Maybe he was dying. Maybe Frank Slate had done a better job than he ever knew. Then again, he might not be sick at all; she was up there, alone with him and there was no telling what they were doing.

Carlyle put the telescope away and sat there in the darkness, thinking of the time old man Snyder had been on his deathbed; she hadn't stayed out at his place more than a few hours at a time.

He began to get a little angry.

Angry at her for being a foolish woman and failing to see the good sense of giving up her ridiculous role as a doctor, and angry at Shaw Dance, who was nothing and had nothing, and yet was more attractive to her than he was. Carlyle found this intolerable.

Finally he got up, put on his coat and hat and went to town.

At Hanley's place, he bought a drink and took it to one of the tables. He saw Max Bucher sitting alone and walked over to him. He didn't like Bucher either, but at the moment he disliked him less than anyone else in the room.

"Do you mind?" Carlyle asked, then sat down before Bucher could answer to let him know that he didn't care if he minded or not.

Bucher was a stubby, bearded man with an accent, which made men distrust him at first. He was in his fifties and never talked about himself, yet he knew the value of a dollar and how to pile one on top of the other.

Carlyle said, "Don't you like to talk?"

"I've got nothing against it," Bucher said. He studied Carlyle from beneath the thicket of his eyebrows. "I've seen happier men than you, Roe. Maybe you ought to get drunk once and forget it all."

"Don't be ridiculous," Carlyle said. "Where were you the other night when Dance brought Frank back?"

46

"Home in bed."

Carlyle frowned. "I don't understand you, Max. You need the timber on Dance's mountain, and you have as much to gain by his dying as I have, or maybe a lot more. You know how much timber is there, and I can only speculate as to the amount of gold."

Bucher sighed. "Sometimes, when I look at that mountain and see the timber on the slopes, I get sick knowing it ain't mine. But what good would it do me if he was dead? All I'd get would be the right to stampede up there with the others and fight you and Slate for a share."

"Just his being dead would satisfy me," Carlyle said bitterly.

Bucher studied him, then laughed. "Ain't she come back yet, Roe?"

"You watch what you say to me, you fat Dutchman." He reached out and gripped Bucher's arm tightly. For a moment, Bucher just looked at the hand gripping him, then he reached into his coat pocket and brought out a large, bone-handled jackknife.

With surprising dexterity he flipped open the broad blade with his fingernails, and in a voice that remained even and unconcerned, he said, "Roe, turn loose of my arm or I'll cut your fingers off."

Roe Carlyle jerked his hand back, surprised by the coldness of Bucher's statement. He looked at the fat man, then said, "You cold-blooded bastard."

"I don't take liberty with you. So don't take it with me. You're mad because the woman's with Dance. He's better than you; can't you see that? Besides, he's been hurt."

"I'm not simple minded," Carlyle snapped. "Damn it, I know what's going on! She's thirty and she's a woman without a man."

"Be careful how loud you say that," Bucher cautioned. "She has friends in Summit who wouldn't like it."

Roe Carlyle smiled. "You, Max? Hell, you've never taken anyone's side in your life."

"That's true, and I don't stay awake at night worrying about my enemies either. People like me, Roe, because I'm a fat Dutchman who works hard and saves his money and keeps his nose out of other people's business." He scratched his beard and folded up his jackknife. "It must be a puzzle to you, trying to understand how a man with your looks and position couldn't make time with Doc Meer. You must be using the wrong approach."

"What the hell would a bachelor know

about it?"

"Not much, but I'll bet you talked about yourself. Shaw Dance talks about her. There's a big difference there."

"A woman's got no business being a doctor," Carlyle said.

Max Bucher chuckled. "A little while ago you was complaining that she had no right to be a woman either. Can't you make up your mind?"

"See! You think she's up there for the same reason that I. . . ."

"I hardly think that's likely," Bucher said quickly. "And you'd better keep this idea of yours to yourself." He got up. "I think I'll get another drink." He went over to the bar and had his glass topped again, but he found a man there to chat with. Roe Carlyle waited, and, when he got tired of sitting alone, he got up also. Bucher timed it right, tossed off his drink and said goodnight just as Carlyle reached the bar.

Bucher paused outside on the walk to look through the window and saw Roe Carlyle gathering listeners, and Bucher shook his head sadly; the fool didn't know when to keep his mouth shut. Carlyle was probably quoting as gospel that which he knew nothing about, but that was his business, not Bucher's.

49

He saw Roan Gentry sitting on his hotel porch and crossed over; Gentry toed a chair around and this was his invitation to sit.

"What's happening that's worth talking about?" Gentry asked. "Carlyle figured a way to get Dance off the mountain?"

"He's sore because the doc's up there," Bucher said.

"Roe's just not enough man for her," Gentry said. "She needs a man who's strong enough to where he don't have to boss her around to prove it." A buggy came down the street and both men turned their heads. As the rig passed in front of the lamplight cast from store windows, they could see that it was Jane Meer, and Gentry put two fingers in his mouth and inelegantly whistled her to the curb.

She stopped by the porch, but didn't get out of the rig.

"How's Dance?" Bucher asked.

"He's over his fever. Tomorrow he'll be moving around." She looked from one to the other. "Are you gentlemen interested in his health?"

"I always liked the boy," Gentry said frankly. "A good independent mind there. We can always use that."

Jane Meer laughed. "Is that why we're friends, Roan?"

"I guess it is," Gentry admitted. Then his manner changed. "Better get on home."

"What?" she asked.

It was too late for him to explain for Roe Carlyle came out of Hanley's, saw her, and crossed the street. He wore a stern frown. "And how is the patient, doctor?"

"He'll be on his feet tomorrow," she said. "Now would you mind stepping back, or do you want me to run over your toes?"

Carlyle grabbed the spoke of the off wheel and held it. "I'm not through talking yet, Jane."

She held the reins and looked at him. "Then say it and let me go home. I'm tired."

"I don't like to see you do things that will start talk," Carlyle said.

Max Bucher chuckled. "Now, who'd be talking, Roe?"

He pointed to Bucher. "I'd remain out of this if I were you."

"You ain't and I guess we both ought to be glad." He got up and left the porch and walked around the buggy and began to crowd Carlyle with his bulk. When he got him clear of the rig, Jane Meer drove on down the street.

Carlyle was furious. "Don't do that to me again!" Then he strode rapidly away.

From the porch, Roan Gentry said,

"Mighty strange and pecky man, ain't he? You've got to watch the ones who pout when they don't get their way." He hoisted himself out of his chair. "Got some good whiskey, Max. Like a snort before bedtime?"

"I have nothing against it," Bucher said and went into the hotel with Gentry.

Shaw Dance felt well enough to sit on his porch after Jane Meer left; she had taken the trail down just before sunset and he calculated that she would reach the town road before full dark. He left the lamp burning and the door open, yet he sat in the deeper shadows for habit was strong with him. He listened to the whir of insects and watched the fireflies dart brightly about. Then he heard the unmistakable click of a Colt hammer being drawn back and before he could move, a woman said, "If you so much as twitch, I'll kill you."

"Why don't you show yourself?" Dance asked. "I don't get many callers and I like to know who they are."

"Stand up," she ordered. "Slowly. Now walk inside. Reach for your rifle and it will be your last move."

"I'm in no hurry to die," Shaw Dance said and did as he was told. When he reached the center of the room, he turned and saw her, a young girl not yet twenty, and for a moment he did not recognize her. Then the dark hair and the gray, Slate eyes, and the straight way she had of standing told him who she was. And from past years came a recollection of her, a thin girl in pigtails, the shy sister to the gallivanting Slate boys.

"Do I have to tell you who I am, Shaw?"

"No," he said. "I recognize you now, Noreen. I haven't seen you for some years."

"I know. Ma doesn't come to town often, and I don't go in without her. I guess we just missed each other." She held the gun on him, as steady as any man. She wore a pair of blue jeans, probably Leed's, and a plaid shirt; her clothes were dusty from a slow, careful climb in the pass.

She backed up until she could touch his rifle, then she worked the lever and spilled the cartridges on the floor until it was empty. Then she kicked the gun away from her.

"I guess I've done what Frank couldn't do," she said.

"You haven't done it yet," Dance said. "Not until you pull that trigger."

"I'm not going to lose another brother to you," she said. "I ain't saying that Frank was right, coming here like he did, but I won't lose another one."

Shaw Dance looked at her steadily, then

leaned back against the table. "You must have quite a life, cooped up in that big house, with servants to wait on you and nice clothes to wear. I'll bet you and your ma have tea every afternoon and stay in the upstairs of the house so that all the man-meanness doesn't touch you."

"It's not your affair how we live!"

"Sure, real gentle ladies. Hate all this rough life, don't you? But you're here now with a gun in your hand, just like any other Slate, ready to kill. Have you asked yourself why? I'll tell you. You're a Slate and the meanness runs deep and a woman's body don't hide it."

"That's a lie!"

"You love your father and brothers. What does it matter to you that they're bigoted and greedy? What difference does it make that Morey's already killed two men over common women? They're Slates, so they must be right. I ain't a Slate, so I've got to be wrong." He glanced at the gun. "Go ahead and squeeze off. Then go home and dress up in a fancy gown and play the piano and sip tea and all the time think about being a Slate, about being as cold and unfeeling as the rest of the Slates. Hell, it's plain to see how you'll be twenty years from now, fat and rough talking, running the Slate empire with a cigar in your mouth."

She began to cry. "I'm not! I'm not that way!"

He took the gun away from her by simply lifting it out of her hand; he laid it on the table and put his arm around her. "Sit down. Come on." He went to the stove for the coffee pot and got a cup for her and made her drink some of it. Then he took a chair across from her and let her compose herself. Dance smiled gently and held her hand. "Noreen, when you came here, you forgot that I knew you when you were a little girl."

"I didn't forget," she said.

"I'm talking about the little girl who bawled at calf branding. The little girl who wanted to nurse every hurt the human race is afflicted with. I couldn't believe that you'd changed that much."

She shook her head and wiped her eyes, then looked at the pistol. "Would you unload that for me, please? It might go off." He picked it up and opened the cylinder and only one cartridge fell out. She smiled shyly. "I was afraid to put more in; I might have shot myself." She brushed her hand across her forehead. "When I thought about coming here — when I knew I had to come here, I wasn't sure how you would be. When

I was ten, you always forgave the fact that I was a Slate, and you were good to me. I didn't know how you'd be now, that's all."

"Do you think I killed Frank in hate?"

She shook her head. "I don't know, Shaw. I guess he hated you. They all do. I don't understand them at all anymore."

"I do," he said. "They hate me because a bastard is supposed to stay a bastard. I'm supposed to swamp out the saloon and pitch feed sacks for a living. If I did that, the Slates would leave me alone."

"There has to be more than that."

"Why, because you can't believe anyone could have so small a reason?" He smiled and shook his head. "I'd better take you on down the mountain. The pass can be dangerous at night if you don't know the way."

"I came up while it was light and hid in the rocks, waiting for her to leave." She glanced at him, then looked at her folded hands. "I've been stupid again, haven't I?" Her laughter was soft. "I got caught in a bog hole once, remember? The fawn was stuck and I just couldn't stand there and do nothing. Why do I always try to straighten out things that can't be straightened out?"

He laughed with her. "You were a mess, mud from head to foot. If that fawn had broken free he'd have hurt you with those sharp hooves. I guess there's a bit of prophesy in it, Noreen. You try to do good and get hurt by it." He got up and went to the stove and stirred the fire. "I'll fix you something to eat."

"No, I'll do it," she said and touched his arm to move him out of the way. When he winced, she was instantly sorry, and saddened. "See? I even hurt you then."

He turned her so that she looked straight at him. "Understand something. I always thought you were the only Slate worth saving." He turned for the water pail and started for the door. "I'll get some water," he said and went out.

At noon, Max Bucher drove to town to pick up his payroll from the bank, and from the clerk he heard how Jane Meer had spent two nights with Shaw Dance, and then acted as though nothing had happened.

It was an ugly thing to hear, told that way, and Bucher left the bank in a disturbed frame of mind. He stopped in at Hanley's for a drink and found an unusually large crowd there; they were laughing and joking about something, but quieted and remained that way until he left.

He had payday to contend with and returned to his mill, but in the early afternoon

57

he got in his buggy and drove back to town. A crowd was congregated in front of Hanley's and Bucher immediately grasped the tone of it; he had heard that vicious muttering sound before, with the hysterical undercurrent ominous and full of danger. Someone talked about getting a fire going to heat some tar, while another speculated on whether or not he should go over to the hotel for a feather pillow.

Bucher wheeled his buggy and drove down an alley and stopped in back of the store. He went in and found Reilly at his counter, his heavy face drawn with concern.

"Damn fools," Reilly said. "They'll all be sorry tomorrow."

"It's today, not tomorrow that I'm thinking of," Bucher said. "We ought to stop it."

"Do you think you could?" He shook his head.

"Give me your shotgun," Bucher said quickly.

Reilly hesitated, then laid the sawed-off on the counter. "Better stay out of it, Max."

"I can't," Bucher said. "I just can't."

He went and got in his rig, but by the time he reached the main street the crowd had moved on. He knew where they were going and went there. They were gathered in front of Jane Meer's house, a noisy, half wild bunch, and Bucher's heart quickened at the sound of it. He boldly drove his buggy to the rearward fringe of the gathering and said, "What are you doing here?"

Two men turned on him and murmured something about minding his own business, and it angered Bucher to be ordered about by ruffians; he picked up the shotgun to give him more authority. The two men pounced on him, took the shotgun away from him, broke it over the buggy wheel, and threw the pieces on the ground.

"Now get out of here," one said. "Before we break you."

Bucher was helpless and he knew it; he could only retreat and think this out. Without hesitation he wheeled his buggy down the street, scattering pedestrians, and tore out of town, heading for Shaw Dance's mountain.

He had never been up the trail, and there were spots of it when his heart thumped as the buggy wheels skirted the rim and disaster. And he was driving faster than he dared, faster than he had ever driven before.

As always, when he was in a hurry, he thought he would never reach the summit of the pass. He knew that Dance's cabin was just beyond those two boulders, parked by nature like sentinels to his domain. As

Bucher pressed the rig between them, the right wheel scraped rock and slewed around.

A rifle banged from a higher place and the bullet whined off a rock.

Bucher whoaed to a halt.

"Dance?" He heard his voice bounce around the mountain.

"What do you want, Max?"

"Shaw, you've got to come with me. There's a ruckus at Doc Meer's place."

"What about?" Dance asked.

The echoes fooled Bucher and he couldn't figure out where Dance was speaking from; he kept looking around like some child playing a game. Bucher said, "Roe Carlyle's started talk. I'm not lying to you."

"What's Roe got to say that I'd be interested in?"

Bucher's voice took on a pleading note. "Shaw, he's got a little mind and when she stayed up here, he got to brooding about it. Shaw, I'm telling you the truth!" He waited for Dance to speak, and when he didn't, Bucher said, "I've got no gun and I'm coming on in. If you want to shoot me, you go ahead."

He snapped the reins against the backs of the team and drove in, expecting a bullet to smash through him, but there was none. He pulled into the clearing and wheeled the team around by Dance's porch.

As he hopped down, he saw Dance walking toward him; Bucher still didn't know where the man had been hidden. There was no particular friendliness in Dance's eyes, but he wasn't pointing his Winchester at Bucher. There was a saddle horse tied up by the lean-to, then Noreen Slate stepped into view.

Bucher could not hide his surprise.

Dance said, "All right, Max, give me the straight of it."

He did, and Dance listened, his expression grave. When he was through, Dance asked, "What made you come to me, Max?"

Bucher seemed a little puzzled about it himself. "Well, I guess it's because you're one man that ain't judged her." He motioned to the buggy. "We don't have any time to lose. We can use my rig."

"All right," Dance said. "Noreen, follow us down." He got aboard Bucher's rig and took the reins and the German seemed relieved. As they rode out of the yard, he said, "I thought you'd kill me when I came through like I did. I can't take much of a scare at my age."

"If you hadn't come on through," Dance said, "I would have been pretty well convinced that you were lying." He held his rifle between his knees and Bucher clung to the seat as Dance drove rapidly down the trail. He plunged through dangerous corners, the wheels often sliding to the sheer drop edge.

"Where's Butler?" Dance shouted.

"Didn't see him," Bucher yelled. "I only thought of you, Shaw, and of her."

"I'll remember that," Dance said, "and that you came to get me."

"Didn't expect to see the Slate girl," Bucher said.

"Neither did I when she showed up. She intended to kill me."

Bucher shot him a quick glance. "She must have changed her mind." Then he closed his eyes, no longer able to sit there and see the buggy slide about the road. And Shaw Dance yelled at the horses to make them go faster.

3

Summit's main street was nearly vacant when Dance and Bucher rushed through and made a skidding turn onto the side street where Jane Meer lived. A huge crowd was still blocking the narrow street in front of her house and Shaw Dance gave no indication of slowing down. He kept the horses at a wild run, heading straight for the men gathered there. Women and children lined both sides of the street and they yelled the warning that saved some lives.

The crowd blocking Dance's way seemed to mash together enough to let the team through, although one person was bowled over by the horses. He hit the fence with the buggy sliding, crashed through and stopped. Then he stood up and faced them before any man could do a thing about it.

When he looked at them he saw the men he knew, and he understood them better than they understood themselves. The hot tar bucket steamed and spread an aroma over the block and one man stood there clutching a feather pillow to his chest. Dance singled out the leaders, the men in the front row; the others didn't count for they had come to see the show and to make noise because it was the thing to do. The front windows of Jane Meer's house were shattered from thrown rocks; boldness against a woman was a thing that had to be worked up slowly. He knew all this from first hand knowledge, and it raised in him an anger that always lay dormant beneath the surface of his consciousness.

His presence, so sudden and so forbidding, brought silence, and he cocked his rifle, the action ringing clearly. Bucher swore later that he could hear the long brass cartridge whisper against the chamber as it went into place.

Then quite matter of factly, Shaw Dance said, "Who'll be the first to step up and die?" He looked at each man in the front row, singling out four of Roe Carlyle's men. "You there. What good are you?" Then he spoke to Bucher without turning his head. "Go on inside, Max, and see if everything's all right. And Max, if she's hurt, you come and tell me. I'm going to hurt somebody then."

The back fringes of the crowd began to stir restlessly, and a few just turned and walked away. Dance looked at the man clutching the feather pillows, and without warning, he shot him point blank. The impact of the bullet knocked the man back into the arms of others, and a moan of horror went up from the crowd. Then the man who had been knocked down slowly got to his feet and inspected himself, surprised that he was still alive. Everyone started to talk at once, and the man who had been holding the pillows yelled once and began to flail a path to safety.

One of Roe Carlyle's men said, "Cute trick, Shaw. The feathers stopped the bullet. You want to try and make me leave?"

Dance jumped down from the buggy and snatched up the bucket of hot tar. He gave it two whirls around his head, and the men packed there suddenly bolted for safety. Then he cast it loose and it fell in the street, some of the tar splashing those a little tardy in leaving.

A few of the trouble makers remained, held there by pride and no small amount of courage. Dance pointed his rifle at them and said, "We'll wait until Max comes back."

The one who had spoke before said, "Why the hell don't we rush him. He can't get us all."

"He may get me," another said. "And I wouldn't like that."

Max Bucher came out of the house and said, "Everything's all right, Shaw." He looked at the men standing there. "It ain't often that I see such brave men."

"Get out of here," Dance advised. "Don't waste time about it."

He waited until they moved away, then he turned and went into the house. Jane Meer was in the parlor, sitting on the sofa. She had a pan of water and a cloth and was pressing it to her forehead, and blood was coloring the water a bright pink. Dance turned to Bucher.

"You lied to me, Max."

"Yes I did. If I hadn't, you'd have killed somebody out there." He turned to the door. "You don't need me now, Shaw."

He went out before Dance could say anything, and when he closed the door, a shard of glass that had been stubbornly clinging to the putty fell and broke.

Dance looked at the lump on Jane Meer's forehead and noticed a welt on her arm. He reached out with his foot and swept some of the broken glass against the baseboard, thus relieving his anger.

She said, "I didn't know you'd come off your mountain for anyone, Shaw."

"I told you I didn't think of you as a doctor."

She looked at him steadily. "I wondered if that was what you meant." She wrung out the cloth and laid it on a small table. "They all have dirty little minds."

"You hate them now? Still?"

"I guess so." She rubbed her bruised arm. "Why did Bucher go for you? What made him know you'd come back with him?"

"Bucher remembers the good people in Summit twenty years ago," Shaw Dance said. "There wasn't much here then, but the people were the same, just fewer of them. It was the same kind of minds that didn't mean to rough up a woman then, but they did. All the things they thought just came out one day."

"I never knew about that," Jane said.

"I don't talk about it. But Bucher knows. So does Gentry and Hanley and some of the old timers; they were here then." He sighed and sat down in a straight-backed chair. "My ma was in the store and a couple of women got to talking. I was just a kid and I didn't get the gist of it right off. Anyway, one lost her temper and called ma a slut. Then they just all seemed to want to hit her, as though she represented something they were ashamed of."

"That's a horrible thing," Jane Meer said.

"She never went up town again," Shaw Dance said softly. "And when she died, pa wouldn't let anyone but family come to the funeral. Then he pulled out."

"But you stayed. To get even?"

He shrugged. "We're all trying to get even for something. There's always something, or someone we've got to hurt." He got up and turned to the door.

"Where are you going?"

"To find Roe Carlyle," he said. He started to pick up his rifle, then thought better of it. "I won't need that, I guess." He stepped outside and found children playing in the street. They were rolling the cooling tar into balls with sticks.

Max Bucher had cleared his buggy from the broken fence and he was waiting. Dance said, "Max, will you drive me out to the smelter so that I can see Roe Carlyle?"

"I figured you'd be wanting a ride," Bucher said and turned the rig. As they drove out of town, he said, "I couldn't find Cove Butler, so I asked around. Carlyle called him to the smelter earlier and he hasn't come back yet."

"I didn't think Cove would have ducked this if he'd known about it," Dance said.

They turned off at the smelter road and followed it; Bucher parked by the main office building and got down when Shaw Dance did. "If you got no objection," he said, "I'll go in with you."

Carlyle was in his office, and Butler was with him. They were examining some reports and Carlyle seemed annoyed to find Dance standing in his doorway.

"I didn't hear you knock," he said. He looked at Bucher. "What are you doing here? I thought you didn't like me."

"That's right," Bucher said. "And I like you less right now."

Cove Butler glanced from one to the other and frowned. "What's going on here that I

68

ought to know about?" He took a cigar from his pocket and bit off the end. "Roe and I were discussing some small thievery."

"That's interesting," Dance said. "And while you were socializing some toughs tried to wreck Jane Meer's place. Did you know about that, Roe?"

"How could I know? I've been here since early this morning."

"You did your talking before that," Bucher said. "I heard some of it, about how Doc Meer wasn't fit to touch a man's wife and kids after she'd bedded up with a man. It all comes back to you, Roe. And I guess it could be proved if we dug deep enough."

"Now wait a minute," Butler said. "Roe, you know I won't stand for any hanky-panky. From you or anyone else."

"I don't have to listen to these accusations," Carlyle snapped.

Dance hadn't come to talk and he started for Carlyle, who looked as though he had suddenly taken root. Then he snatched open a drawer and darted a hand inside for his revolver. Dance wasn't close enough to reach him, so he kicked out and slammed the drawer shut on Carlyle's hand. He yelped and backed away, and Cove Butler stepped between them.

Max Bucher said, "I ain't no fighter, but

since he's got a bum hand, that'll make us even." Butler couldn't hold Dance and stop Bucher too, so Bucher moved around the desk and hit Roe Carlyle. He snapped him back, drove him into a small assayer's table, which toppled and spilled scales and crucibles onto the floor.

"Butler! Stop him!"

"Stop him yourself," Butler said and opened the door. "Let me know how Max makes out, Shaw." He went on down the hall.

Carlyle was standing against the wall, clutching his injured hand and bleeding from Bucher's blow on the mouth. Then he realized that the fight was his and charged the fat German. They met in a collision and traded a half dozen blows, but it was Carlyle who gave way; he could not budge the stubborn determination that was in Bucher.

Catching Carlyle over the heart, Bucher drove him to his knees, then stood there and waited for the man to get up.

Dance saw that Carlyle was through, and he said, "Why don't you let him go, Max? You're not going to get enough of a fight out of him to bother with."

"He's got to get up sometime," Bucher said, panting heavily.

Carlyle looked at them. "Dance, everyone's scared of your gun and your fists. But there's more than one way to lick a man and I'm just getting started on you."

"Poor start," Bucher said simply.

"And I'll get you, you lard belly!" He grasped the edge of a desk. "There's more to me than you'll ever be, Bucher."

"A point for argument there," Dance said. "Roe, I take one look at you and see all there is to see. And there ain't enough there to make a second look worth while."

"A blind man can't see anything," Carlyle spat out. "And you're a blind man, Shaw. You sit up there on your mountain and think no one can touch you. Well I can touch you when I want to. I know how to bring you down, Shaw." He laughed. "Don't think you'll take her up there with you. She wouldn't go. She's got a pride like yours, Shaw, and she wants to make the town sorry for the way it's acted."

"Let's get out of here," Bucher said. "He makes me sick."

"Yeah, go on, get out," Carlyle said and painfully got to his feet.

Shaw Dance paused in the doorway. "Leave her alone from now on, Roe."

Bucher paused by his buggy. "The first man I ever fought with my fists. He wasn't much, but I guess I whipped him, didn't I?"

71

"You did all right, Max." He got in the rig and sat there, holding his bad arm in his lap.

Bucher said, "You look a little peaked, Shaw. Kind of overdone it, didn't you?"

"I'm all right," Dance said. He turned and looked at Bucher. "Max, you've been looking at the mountain for some years now. I've probably got twenty years of cutting there, including the south flank."

"It's a fact," Bucher said, starting the team in motion. "But I'm not going to ask you and I ain't going to kill you for it."

"That's something I wasn't sure of until today," Dance said. "Roe's right; he can bring me down when he wants to now. He knows how. But I'm going to save him the trouble, Max. I'm going to be a town man."

Bucher frowned. "She means that much to you?"

"Seems that she does," Dance said. "Max, do you want to go into the timber business with me, partners?"

This had long been a dream of Bucher's, to get his fallers into that timber. Still he remained calm, sober about it. "I'd like it fine, Shaw, but you don't owe me anything. Nothing at all."

"I trust you, Bucher."

This flattered the fat German and for a

few minutes he was too overcome to speak. "You want to draw up some papers on it?"

"Best if it's legal."

"It's all right with me, a handshake, I mean. But what about your mine? When the word gets out that you're not roosting up there, every man who owns a shovel will be up there."

"A few sticks of dynamite will close the shaft," Dance said. "Then too, I'll be on the mountain a good deal of the time, once we start pushing in a road and falling. It's still my mountain, Max, and they know it."

"It must be nice," Bucher said, "to have a place where no one can touch you."

"Who has?" Dance asked. "I thought I had, then I kept remembering a woman's smile and all I had to know was that she needed help."

"Be sure and tell her that," Bucher said. "She needs to hear it, Shaw. She needs to know she's a woman."

"She knows it," Dance said. "Let me off at her place. I'll see you in your lawyer's office in an hour."

"I never thought the day would turn out like this," Bucher said. "I sure didn't."

"Casting bread upon the waters," Dance said and got out at the corner. He watched Bucher turn around and drive away, then he walked on to Jane Meer's house. She was nailing boards over her broken windows and she put the hammer down when Shaw Dance came down the walk.

"Do you feel better for having hurt Roe?"

He frowned. "I didn't hurt him. Max Bucher hit him a couple of times."

"Come on in," she said and led the way into the house. She had swept the broken glass into piles and picked up some of it in a dustpan. "I've made some coffee."

While she put out the cups, he studied her. The bruise on her head was ugly and he knew that it pained her severely, but she seemed to ignore it. "Jane, I'm going to live in town part of the time. Max and I are going into the timber business together."

"Why?"

"Why am I moving to town? Or going into partnership with Max?"

"Moving to town."

He smiled. "Because I can't think of you as a doctor, and can't stop thinking of you as a woman." He moved to her and put his arm around her, then kissed her. She remained in his arms for a short time, then impatiently pushed herself away.

"Don't ask me to change what I am, Shaw."

"I wasn't going to. Jane, we'd make out all

74

right, you and I."

"Yes. Yes, I know." She poured the coffee, then sat across from him. "I can't make up my mind whether or not I love you, Shaw. I don't think that I really know what it is. If it's putting aside what I want for what you want, then I don't love you. I couldn't be that unselfish. Could you accept me on those terms, Shaw?"

"Sure. You're getting no bargain yourself."

He remained better than a half hour, and when he left, he felt a vague disappointment, for in his mind this was more than an agreement, an arrangement, a bargain struck. Yet Jane Meer seemed to treat it unemotionally, while he could not, and it made him wonder if there was not some basic, insoluble difference between them.

Max Bucher was waiting in front of the attorney's office, and he and Dance went in together. Lyle Harler was working on a legal brief, but he put this aside and waved Bucher and Dance into chairs.

"To see either of you in my office doesn't surprise me," Harler said softly. "But together, it must be coincidence."

"We're together," Shaw Dance said.

"All right," Harler said. "What is it?"

Bucher glanced at Shaw Dance, then said,

"We want to draw up partnership papers, Lyle."

It was Harler's business to deal with unusual elements, but this surprised him and he didn't bother to hide it. For a moment he just stroked his mustache and looked from one to the other, then drew paper and pen toward him. "Let me have the facts."

This took longer than Dance had anticipated; he spent two hours in Harler's office until every detail was taken care of. In the end, Bucher was to supply the labor and sawing equipment and meet the payroll while Dance shared the cost of improving the road halfway up the mountain. This was introduced in the general agreement since Dance engaged in mining, and should he choose to haul ore over the road, it would not be fair that Bucher should pay for it and get no profit from it.

With the agreement signed, they went across the street to Hanley's for a drink. Dance bought and he and Bucher bellied up to the bar.

"Won't take this long to get around town," Bucher said. "May be a good thing at that. I can put on thirty men tomorrow. A hundred by the end of the month. Now if we can ever get the railroad through the valley, we'll make a fortune."

"Christian Slate can't hold out forever," Dance said. "He's the only man in Nevada who's content to drive to market."

"He ain't content," Bucher said. "Just stubborn."

Horsemen pulled up to the hitchrail out front with a flurry of dust and sound and Bucher turned his head to see who it was.

"Talk of the devil," he said, and Christian Slate came in, followed by his three sons.

They made straight for Dance and Max Bucher, and then Morey kicked Dance's rifle out of reach and Christian Slate pulled his pistol. "Come along, Dance."

"You old fool," Dance said softly, "you can't pull this in broad daylight."

"Morey, if he speaks again, or resists, strike him on the head with your pistol."

"Yes, pa."

Bucher said, "What is this anyway?"

Turning to him, Christian Slate said, "I have nothing against you, Bucher. Stay clear of this. It's a personal matter between myself and Dance. And I hate the thought of it as much as any man can."

He stepped back then and motioned to the door. Dance looked at Bucher, then said, "As soon as we're gone, go get Cove Butler."

"You won't need the law," Christian Slate said. "No harm will come to you, Dance, unless you kick up a fuss." His nod was enough to get them moving and they stepped to the walk, Morey behind Dance, and Kyle and Leed on either side. The old man holstered his pistol and led the way down the street.

They turned off toward the church, then the old man opened the gate leading to the parsonage and held it open for them to pass through. Dance hesitated, but Morey shoved him on, then they went inside.

Noreen Slate was in the parlor, crying, and the minister was with her, a thin man, nervous at best, and now highly distressed. He said, "God forbids such a thing!"

"You have me to contend with before you meet God," Christian Slate said flatly. "There's no need to delay. Read the words, preacher."

"Now just a minute!" Dance said. "What is this?"

"A wedding," Christian Slate said. "Dance, you'll not blight my daughter with your bastardly ways. She confessed to me finally that she remained a night in your cabin."

"I didn't want her taking a spill on the trail," Dance said. "She'll tell you that!"

"Yes," the old man said. "She's told me that. I also know that she went there to kill you and did not. The cause that stopped her finger on the trigger makes a lie of what else she might say." His face was dark with an anger magnificently suppressed. "Dance, I would rather have her married to a drunk, a horse thief, a man about to be hung, than to you. I raised her to be a lady, and she chooses trash. So be it. All right, preacher, say what has to be said."

"I protest," the man said feebly.

Morey spoke up softly. "One more time, friend, and you're going to protest with a sore head." He reached out and grabbed his sister by the arm and pulled her to her feet, then shoved her against Shaw Dance. "Now splice 'em, and do a first class job of it."

Noreen Slate looked at Dance, and said, "I'm sorry. Please don't hate me."

He stared stonily ahead as though he had not heard her, or wasn't even conscious that she stood at his side.

The minister began the ceremony, and when it came to the responses, neither Dance nor the girl would speak. Christian said, "They do. Get on with it."

"But Mr. Slate, they're supposed to respond."

"I'm responding for them," the old man

79

said. "Don't make me tell you again."

The minister hesitated, then went on and finished the ceremony. He started to tell the groom that he could kiss the bride, but thought better of it and fell silent.

"All right, boys," Christian Slate said. "Take 'em outside."

They went to the porch, then halfway down the walk. "That's far enough," the old man said. He pointed to the buckboard tied to the hitching post. "I give you that. Your baggage is loaded, all you own. And I'll give you him when I'm finished." He swung around and hit Shaw Dance flush in the mouth, driving him back into Morey's arms. "All right, boys, have your fun."

Leed hit first because he had been holding it back a long time, and he opened a cut on Dance's face. There was no defense to be made; he kept striking out, hoping to hurt them a tenth as much as they hurt him. He was like a ball passed from man to man, not thrown back, but struck back, and only some inner will kept him on his feet, kept pushing strength into his legs.

Cove Butler came running down the street and Christian Slate said, "Let him fall," and they backed away and Dance fell on his face and lay still.

As Butler came through the gate, he said,

"The whole bunch of you are under arrest."

"For what?" Morey asked. "We was just having a little shivaree after the wedding and things got out of hand." He grinned. "Dance ain't used to our ways yet."

"What wedding?" Butler asked.

"My daughter just became Dance's wife," Christian Slate said. "Do you want to put your nose into a family affair, sheriff?"

"I'm going to look into this," Butler said.

"Fine, you do that." The old man stood there and then Butler turned and went back up town. When he looked at his daughter, he found her kneeling, holding Dance's head in her lap; she was wiping his face with the hem of her dress. A brightness came into the old man's eyes. "In spite of your tears and denials, I see that I came to the heart of the truth after all. When my daughter holds the head of a man like that, I've lost her. And good riddance."

Tears ran down her cheeks and she brushed them angrily away. "Yes, I love him," she said. "I knew that when I left the mountain. And I had a hope that maybe — but you've killed that for me now. You've tied him to me, a woman he doesn't want. And he'll hate me because I'm a Slate."

"You'll be a fitting pair," Christian Slate said flatly. "Go with him. Take him home;

it's your home now. And when he comes around, tell him to care for you well or I'll put a Slate brand on him he'll wear the rest of his life." He started to turn away, then thought of another thing. "Tell him also to name none of the brats any name connected with Slate."

They left her in the yard with Dance, and, when they passed on down the street, the minister came out, wringing his hands and uttering moans of sympathy.

With his help she got Dance into the buckboard and then mounted it and drove out of town, taking the alleys so that fewer people would see them. She didn't care about herself. It was Dance she thought of, for the shame was his to bear, and since he was blameless, the matter became all the more acute.

They were well up the mountain road before Dance regained full consciousness, and then he tried to sit up, slipped and fell off the buckboard. She stopped and jumped down and tried to help him but he pushed her away from him so hard that she almost went down. Slowly, painfully, he got to his feet. One eye was puffed and closed, and his lower lip was split and still bleeding a little.

He looked at her steadily for a full minute,

then said, "If you ever touch me, I'll hit you."

She came over to him, close to him, yet not touching him. "Hit me now," she begged. "Beat me. Hurt me as I've hurt you. Please." He saw the tears come, saw the pain in her eyes, and without thought he folded her in his arms and held her while she cried. "Shaw, what have I done to you? What have I done?"

4

Max Bucher drove up the mountain the next day and found Shaw Dance living in the lean-to barn. For a moment, Bucher simply stared at Dance, then got down from his buggy, saying, "You've taken a beating, as bad as I've seen and still be able to walk." He looked around, and gave particular attention to the cabin.

"She's inside," Dance said.

Bucher nodded. "Married, huh? Too bad. A thing like marriage shouldn't start like this."

"I didn't want it," Dance said. "She didn't want it, but it couldn't be stopped. The old bull was just going to have his way."

"And one of these days you'll have yours?"

"That's right," Dance said solemnly. "I'm

not going to sleep good until his fences are down and the tumbleweeds are blowing across his deserted yard." He changed the subject quickly. "When does road building commence?"

"Right away," Bucher said. "That's what I came to talk to you about."

To save time and money, Bucher wanted to build only a half mile of good road, near the lower portion of the mountain, then start eating a way through the timber, building as they went. It suited Dance, and after Bucher drove back to town, Dance went back to the lean-to; it was hardly a livable place and he wanted to improve it.

Then too, it kept him away from the cabin; he didn't want to go inside, or to look at her because he was sorry she had to endure this relationship, sorry it made her cry.

She came out of the cabin at noon and said, "Dinner's on the table."

He didn't pause in his work or look at her. "Put the plate outside."

"You're not a dog! Eat at the table like a man!"

He threw his hatchet down and faced her. "Your old man made it plain what I am. And you're a Slate."

Her expression firmed. "Your plate's on

the table. Eat it there or starve." She turned and went back to the cabin.

He was stubborn enough to pass up the noon meal and live with his hunger, and stubborn enough not to come when he was called for supper. He waited until he figured she was through eating, then went to the house and found her sitting at the table, patiently waiting for him.

Dance ate in silence, then when she picked up the dishes to carry them to the sink, he said, "It strikes me as being foolish that I should sleep in the barn when I've got a wife in the house." She stopped and stood there, partially turned to him, yet not looking at him. "It only seems fair that since I've had a wife pushed off on me that I treat her like a wife."

"Would you do that to me, Shaw?" She turned and faced him. "Do you think for a minute that you could hurt my father by hurting me?"

He slammed his fist down on the table. "Damn it, don't I have the right to hurt him?" He made a cutting motion with his hand and got up. "You don't have to be afraid of me, Noreen."

"I'm not afraid of you," she said. She was, he thought, a pretty girl. Her face was rather square and her nose short and straight.

Then he didn't want to look at her anymore and went out, taking the shame he felt with him.

Dance spent the next sixteen days with Max Bucher and the crew grading and cutting out the road. He arrived on the job in the early morning and stayed with it until sundown, then he went back up the mountain to his cabin where Noreen had his supper waiting.

They didn't talk much; every time he thought of something to say he remembered that she was his wife under protest, and the hate for Christian Slate came to him so strong that he could not risk speaking, could not risk taking it out on her.

He wished he could help her, tell her that he held her blameless, but he couldn't find the words. Perhaps there weren't any words.

Dance went to town on some business that Bucher couldn't take time off to attend to, and, after taking care of it, he walked to Jane Meer's house and knocked on the door. She had a patient, so he waited in the parlor, and finally she came out, wiping her hands on a towel.

"You don't look like a happy bridegroom," she said. "Evidently you believe in short engagements."

He looked steadily at her. "I thought you'd

know, and understand. Surely you heard how it happened."

"Of course I heard, but what does that change? She's your wife, all nice and legal." She threw the towel into a chair. "And day and night, she's there, in your house, cooking your meals and washing your shirts. Do you think I'm a fool, Shaw? You're as human as any man. How long do you think it'll stay that way?"

"I live in the lean-to."

"My, that's noble." She laughed because she didn't think this was at all funny. "Shaw, she's a woman, young, fairly pretty, and she's a Slate, as hard and as calculating as her father or brothers. And I suspect that she has as few morals."

"That's not fair," he said. "Noreen's a good girl. I've known her since she could walk."

"Oh, sure. And I suppose you're going to tell me she didn't know what she was doing when she stayed the night at your place?"

"I asked her to do that," Dance said. "The trail is tricky at night."

"Which is exactly what she wanted," Jane Meer said. "Shaw, men are always fools where women are concerned. Christian Slate didn't want to lose another son to that mountain, so he traded you a daughter for a share of it." She made a face to show her impatience with him. "Christian Slate bought a new son-in-law and he'll expect something from you, like permission to graze cattle on the lower slopes."

"You're wrong," Dance said, "but I don't suppose I can convince you of it."

"That's right, you can't."

Dance took his hat and put it on a side table. "Jane, I didn't come here to argue with you."

"I know, but I had to say what was on my mind." She looked at him. "What are you going to do, Shaw, stay married to her?"

He shook his head. "A divorce is an ugly thing; you know how people talk about a divorced women. Hanley's wife is divorced, you know, and after being married to Hanley for eleven years, people still speak of it." He frowned. "There's no need to hurt her, Jane. I spoke to Harler and he mentioned something about getting the marriage annulled. It's different from a divorce. An annullment means that a wedding never took place."

"Do you think the swine who live here will make that distinction?" But she patted his arm. "Come on, I've got a pot of coffee on. We'll find something pleasant to talk about."

■ ■ ■ ■

Cove Butler began each day when the sun was high, and he prefaced his work with a walk along main street, to let everyone see that he was on the job, and to have a look at the town, to pinpoint if he could, the sources of mischief that might develop into real trouble.

As he approached the hotel, he saw one of Christian Slate's men sitting on the porch; this was the third day of this idleness, and Butler went on inside the place to see Roan Gentry.

Gentry was paring an apple, his chair leaned against the key pigeonholes. Butler said, "Is she still here?"

"Yep," Gentry said. "Wants to see you. Told me to send you up as soon as you come on duty."

"This is the first time she's been to town in six years," Butler said. "All right, what do I have to lose?" He smiled and went up the stairs, then knocked on a door halfway down the hall.

"Come in."

He stepped inside and took off his hat. "You wanted to see me, Mrs. Slate?"

She turned from the window, a tall, slender woman with iron gray hair and tired eyes. "I saw Shaw Dance come into town," she said. "I would like to speak to him if he will spare me the time."

"I'll fetch him," Butler said and reached behind him for the doorknob. "Mrs. Slate, that wasn't Shaw Dance's doing a few weeks ago."

She nodded. "You don't have to tell me."

"And about Frank —"

"I know my sons," she said. "Please fetch Mr. Dance."

"Yes'm," Butler said and walked down the stairs.

He found Dance coming out of Jane Meer's house, stopped him, spoke briefly, then they walked on to the hotel together. Butler remained in the lobby as Dance went on upstairs. His knock was answered quickly and he stepped into the room.

She had changed considerably, he saw, older now, more worn now. "You're kind to have come," she said.

"Butler tells me you've been here three days. If I'd known —"

"Days don't mean much to me," she said. "Sit down, Shaw. My, it's been some years, hasn't it? You haven't changed though. Still serious in your ways."

"It may be that I had much to be serious

90

about," Dance said.

"Yes, I know. There was a time in this country when the ground shook and the wind blew when my husband walked around. When I was young and the boys were little, it used to make me so proud to see the way people listened to him when he spoke, or turned their heads when he passed. And the times when he took up his gun and killed a man I always said that it was right for the strong to protect what was theirs. Things would change, I always said. By the time the boys were grown, all the wildness would be gone. But that was a woman's foolish hope, Shaw. They took the wildness and carried it along like it was a precious thing they couldn't bear to lose, like they were afraid they couldn't settle anything at all except by violence."

"I'm sorry about Frank," Dance said. "But he came for me, although I don't expect you to understand that."

"Frank always wanted the best piece of meat on the platter, or the biggest piece of cake. It was his way, to grab and take and hold on. Christian taught him that." She looked steadily at Dance, her expression sad. "You know you could have stopped all this? Saved us all this? So easy too. If you'd only lived a little in awe of them or got off

91

the walk when you saw them coming." She shook her head. "But of course you couldn't do that, could you?"

"No," he said. "I'm sorry to say that I couldn't."

"I didn't come here because of Frank. It's Nori I'm thinking of. Do you treat her well? Forgive me for asking, for even thinking that you might make her pay for the sins of her father."

"She wanted this no more than I," Shaw Dance said. "I wouldn't hurt her."

Mrs. Slate closed her eyes and remained still and silent for a moment. "I guess I can go home now and sleep without worry. If she should ever need me, you'd let me know, wouldn't you?"

"Yes," Shaw Dance said.

"Christian would be against my coming, but he wouldn't stop me. I can be strong, Shaw."

"Ma'am, only a strong woman could have lived with Christian Slate for thirty-five years."

She had no luggage, just her shawl and a cloth handbag, and Dance opened the door for her and gave her his arm while descending the stairs. Butler joined them and they went to the porch where Mrs. Slate spoke to the man lounging there.

He went down to the stable for the buggy while they stood in the shade. While they waited, Kyle Slate rode into town on his blooded horse. He came over to the hotel side and said, "It's about time you're coming home, ma."

"I said I would when I was ready," she said. "I suppose your pa sent you."

"Asking for myself," Kyle said. He looked at Shaw Dance. "I want to see you, Mr. Dance."

"You see me," Dance said.

"Come over to Hanley's," he said and wheeled to cross the street. It was, Dance thought, the Slate way of doing things, to drop an order, cold and terse, and leave it there, knowing that it would be obeyed.

He waited until Mrs. Slate was seated in the buggy, and stood there while she drove out of town.

Butler said, "Care for a drink, Shaw?"

Dance grinned. "Trying to make it easy for me to go over to Hanley's?"

"I've got a bottle of good stuff in my office," Butler said. "Hell, you're looking for an excuse to spit in a Slate's eye, and who am I to deny you?"

Dance laughed and walked on down the street with Butler. The jail was on the corner and Butler unlocked the door and motioned for Dance to take the chair by the desk. He brought out the bottle and two glasses and poured.

Dance drank, then said, "That is good stuff, Cove. What's the occasion?"

Butler shrugged. "Christian Slate expects you to declare war on him, and I was just wondering if you were going to disappoint him or not. Then too, there's a railroad man at the hotel. He says he wants to talk to you, because when you and Bucher get that other saw camp in operation, the railroad would like to handle your business. They've only got forty miles of spur line to lay and they'll run three trains a week."

"Has Slate sold them the valley right of way?"

"No," Butler said. "But the railroad man still wants to talk."

"Talk is cheap," Dance said.

The door slammed open and Kyle Slate stopped there. He looked at Shaw Dance and said, "When I say I want to see a man, he usually comes on the run."

Shaw Dance got up slowly, lazily, then he snatched up the chair he had been sitting in, swung it, and caught Kyle Slate flush in the chest with it. The force of the blow knocked him backward through the open door and onto the sidewalk, and Dance was after him and had him before he could get up, or before Butler could come around the desk.

He hauled Slate inside before he could resist, kicked the door shut with his foot, and relieved Kyle of his six-shooters. Then he shoved him away and said, "The last time you had two brothers to help you. Why, you stupid jackass, don't you know I've been waiting for a chance to get you alone?"

"You won't find it easy picking," Kyle said and bowled into Dance. They hooked punches into each other, then Dance hit Kyle in the Adam's apple, causing him to gag and retreat toward the cell blocks. He went after Kyle with brutal intent, grabbing him by the hair and banging the man's head against the steel bars as though he were using a maul.

Kyle lost consciousness the third time his head struck the steel, yet Dance continued to hold him up and batter him. Butler dashed over to pull Dance away, but he could not.

"You're killing him!" Butler yelled. Dance ignored him and Butler drew his pistol, meaning to hit Dance with it. Yet he hesitated, and said, "Shaw, you'll have to see Mrs. Slate again and tell her you've taken another son from her. How much can she stand?"

It went through him like a saber, and he dropped Kyle Slate and looked at Cove Butler. Then he turned away and shook his head; the wild anger was gone from his eyes and he slumped against the wall.

Butler knelt and turned Kyle Slate's head. Blood matted the hair and back and he felt to see how bad was the damage. "I think we'd better call Doc Meer," he said. "He needs some stitches."

"I'll get her," Dance said.

"You stay here," Butler said and scooped up his hat and went out, clapping it on his head as he hit the sidewalk and turned down the street.

Shaw Dance sat down again and looked at Kyle Slate and was sorry he'd battered the man, sorry because Kyle wasn't the one he wanted to batter. It's the old man I want, he thought, yet somehow he had never come to grips with him. Christian Slate always pushed the work off onto his sons.

Butler returned in a short time, and Jane Meer came in and quickly knelt by Kyle Slate. The man was still unconscious, and she shaved the back of his head, closed the wounds and bandaged him. Butler collared three men off the street and they took the bench in front of the jail, loaded Kyle Slate on it, and carried him to Jane Meer's house, where she kept a three bed ward for hospitalized patients.

She remained behind after Butler and the others had left. "Well, Shaw, I'm beginning to think that you're incapable of talking without a gun or your fists." Then her tone gentled. "I suppose he started it. Every piece of trouble the Slates run into, they start. It's a point of honor with them, I suppose." She snapped her bag closed and turned to the door. "You've made up your mind to declare war on Christian Slate, haven't you?"

"I see no other way," Dance said. "Do you?"

"No. Then make it quick and get rid of *her.* I never liked to wait."

He waited for Butler to return. He came in and closed the door. "I've about made up my mind on the whole lot of you," Butler said. "Before the day's over, I'm going to see Judge Hockett and have you put under a peace bond, you and all the Slates. Then the first one who steps out of line is going to jail."

"You act like it's my fault," Dance said.

"It's half your fault, but I don't propose

to argue it with you. Let's go see the railroad man."

Westbrook Arnold had a two room suite at the hotel, and he invited them in. Arnold was forty, tall, well dressed, and soft spoken; he offered them cigars, a drink, and chairs, then smiled pleasantly at Shaw Dance.

"I've heard about you and your mountain," Arnold said. "You may be wondering why I'm anxious to talk to you instead of Christian Slate, for he does own the property I wish to buy." Arnold shrugged. "It's very simple, really. I can't deal with Slate, so I'll deal with the man strong enough to deny Slate his whims."

Shaw Dance puffed on his cigar, then said, "Mr. Arnold, we just can't do any business at all. Unless you want me to break Christian Slate's back and force him to sell."

"The railroad would never agree to such a thing," Arnold said. "However, if something happened that forced Slate to change his mind, the railroad would be appreciative. Gentlemen, there is no more noble motive than profit. You're in business. We use a lot of ties and timber. Our market would be worth developing, and our rates, to a co-operative firm, would be attractive."

Butler said, "I think the conversation is going to develop into something I hadn't ought to hear." He started to get up, but Arnold waved him back.

"This concerns you, marshal. Hear me out. We're not going to plot, but discuss logically a bad situation." He enumerated his points by holding up one finger at a time. "First, the railroad will be a boon to the town. Regular passenger service twice a week, and freight three times. The mines are solidly behind the building of the line, and Mr. Bucher has spoken to me before and offered his support. Only one man stands in the way of this progress. He's got to go."

"No one will argue that," Dance said.

"But how he goes makes a difference," Cove Butler said. "Damn it, Shaw, the old man's property is his, as the mountain is yours, and the right to keep it or sell it is his decision, as it is yours." He slapped the arms of his chair and got up. "I may not strike you as much, Mr. Arnold, but I won't stand for the railroad messing in the ill feeling between Dance and Slate. It started as a personal matter, and it will stay that way."

"Well and good," Westbrook Arnold said pleasantly. "But you won't deprive the railroad of taking advantage of any opening that presents itself, will you?"

"Not as long as it's legal," Butler said.

"Or what you can prove," Arnold said. "All right, gentlemen, I'll be satisfied with those terms. And we must talk again, Mr. Dance. Soon, I trust."

"We may," Dance said and went out with Cove Butler.

"Men who work just for the money worry me," Butler said when they reached the street.

"You must worry a lot," Dance said. He glanced at Butler. "Are you still going ahead with that peace bond?"

"I guess not," the sheriff said. "It wouldn't really stop either of you, would it?"

"No," Dance said. "Just what are you trying to save, Cove? Me or Christian Slate?"

"The town," Butler said. "I don't suppose you understand that, or even think it's worth the trouble."

"That's about it," Dance admitted. He started to step on down the street, but Butler put out his hand and stopped him.

"Shaw, my wife asked me to mention that we'd like to have you for supper some Sunday evening. I notice your wife doesn't get to town much."

"Under the circumstances, it seems reasonable that she wouldn't."

Butler exposed some of the hard anger he habitually suppressed. "You damned fool, who'd blame her?"

"You want me to point them out to you?" He stared at Butler. "It's a bad business, Cove. Let us settle it our own way." He left the sheriff standing there and got in his rig and drove back to his mountain.

Bucher had already built a mess hall and office building in a clearing and Dance cut off the road and tied the team in front before going in. He found Bucher adding some figures.

When he was finished, Bucher put aside his pencil and turned his chair half around to face Dance. "Transportation is going to eat the biggest hole in the profits. Did you get to see the railroad man?"

"There's a calculating cuss," Dance opined.

Bucher shrugged. "More money was made with the pen than the sword. I'll take a fig-urin' man over a fightin' one anytime." He had a crock of beer on the desk and dipped into it with two teacups; he handed one to Dance. "It's plain to me that if there was real trouble, we could expect some help from the railroad."

"Do you want a war with Christian Slate?"

Bucher shook his head. "I'm no fighter and a worse gambler. I'd be afraid of los-ing."

"I wouldn't," Dance said flatly. "All my life I've been stepped on and pushed by the Slates. Now I'm of a mind to run them right out of the country."

"Be a better place to live," Bucher admitted. "Still, to start a ——"

"Hell, it's been started," Dance snapped. "Damn you, Max, do you have to have all the right on your side? Can't you settle for just a little of it?" He drank some of his beer. "I've been thinking. I saw Noreen's mother in town. The old woman's lonely for her, wants to see her and don't quite dare. But that wouldn't stop me. Suppose I hitch up the buggy and take my 'wife' home to see her mother. Christian won't like it, but I really don't think he'll start trouble over it. It would give me a chance to talk to him."

"What could you say that hasn't been said before?"

Shaw Dance leaned forward and spoke softly. "I could tell him to open up that right of way or get it opened up for him."

Max Bucher drew his breath in sharply. "God, that's a plain declaration of war!"

"Ain't it though?" Dance said and went out and got into his rig. He drove on up the mountain and found Noreen washing clothes in the yard. She stopped work and watched him get down from the buggy, and she gave him a shy smile when he came up.

"You needed shirts and I —"

"That's not important," he said. "Fix your hair and what else you want to do. I'll take you home to visit your ma. Saw her in town and she's lonely for you."

She looked at him and bit her lower lip, then turned and ran into the house. He waited a few minutes, then she came out with a different dress on, and a bonnet in her hand.

As he handed her into the buggy, she said, "You're good to me, Shaw."

"It's nothing," he said and drove off the mountain.

When he reached the town road, he took the south fork. It was a strange feeling, to be driving this road which he had looked at daily from the distant rise of his mountain, yet had never set foot on. Within a mile of the fork he came to a gate in an endless barbed wire fence; he was on Slate land once he passed through, and he had not driven far before he was seen by two riders. They were some distance away, but they swung toward the advancing buggy and pulled alongside without stopping them. Dance could see they were only hands working for wages, and merely following orders; they didn't speak, just sided the buggy all the rest of the way to Christian Slate's ranch house.

As they approached the porch, Christian Slate stepped out and the two riders wheeled and rode out of the yard. Dance stopped and got down. Christian Slate said, "What are you doing on my property?"

Dance ignored him; he handed Noreen down and said, "Your ma's waiting." She hesitated and he gave her a slight shove, then she dashed past the threatening figure of her father and went into the house.

Morey and Leed came from the tack shed, took one look, then trotted across the yard. They stood slightly behind Shaw Dance, just within his range of vision.

"I'm sorry my other boy, Kyle, isn't here," Christian Slate said, "but he went to town earlier and ain't back yet."

"I saw him there," Dance said evenly. "He's at Doc Meer's now, getting his head sewed up." He turned suddenly and faced the two brothers. "Stand around where I can see you good."

"Big talk," Leed said, smiling. "Your rifle's in the buggy."

"Do as he says," Christian said. "It offends me to have an unarmed man threatened on my property. Dance, you've got a gall coming here." Then he frowned. "You

104

and Kyle have words?"

"Very few," Dance said. "He wanted trouble and got it." Dance knew how to talk to this old man; Slate had more than his share of courage and he admired it in others. "There never was a day when your boys could lick me unless one had each arm and the other did the pounding. Kyle wanted to try it on his own, so I obliged him."

"One of these days I'm going to try it alone," Leed said.

This made the old man angry. "You fool kid, he'll whup you proper. Now get on with your work. Sit, Dance, and talk. The women will gabble for an hour at least."

Dance went to the porch and sat down. "First time I ever saw the valley from your porch," he said. "If the railroad ran through here —"

"It don't run through here," the old man said. "Not likely to either."

"They pay good money for the right of way."

"I've got money." He looked at Dance. "And I've heard of injunctions too. Hell, I've got lawyers. Go ahead, get an injunction. By the time I'm through fighting it through the courts, you'll be too old to ride the damned train."

"You'd lose, all down the line," Dance

said. "Why fight it?"

"Because I want to," Slate said. "What other reason does a man have for ever fighting a thing? You forget the nonsense and come right down to the meat of life, and it's pretty simple. A man will always do what he wants to do, and there really ain't no stopping him. Dance, the trouble with you is you don't give folks credit for havin' good sense. Hell, I'm mean and I know it. Don't want to change either. Sometimes I even enjoy it. My old man was mean. Had six sons and gave them all girl's names, so they'd grow up tough."

"That's a hell of a thing to be proud of," Dance said.

The old man snorted. "Who's proud of it? I just said that I am what I am. Same as you. Man, no one ever blamed you because you was a bastard. Hell, we knew it wasn't your fault. Only you never knew your place. As a kid you was proud to the point of sin and you pushed your way in where you didn't belong just to see if you could get away with it. You carried a chip on your shoulder and you got it knocked off. Why cry about it?"

"Slate, I'm not a kid now. So I'll lay it on the line to you. For the good of the town, the railroad's coming through."

The old man laughed. "The good of the town? Ain't you man enough to admit your real reasons? You want the railroad to go through my property because I say it ain't. Hell, it's just another case of your stickin' your nose in where it don't belong."

"That never stopped you from wanting my mountain."

"I don't want your goddamned mountain. I want the cocky man sitting up there who thinks he's better than me. You ain't, Dance, and if I have to kill you to prove it, I will."

Dance held his anger in check. "I figure sixty days is time enough to sell the right of way, Slate."

"Sixty days from now, I won't have changed my mind." He looked at Shaw Dance. "What'll you do, take the land away from me? Hell, I'll have the federal marshal on you."

"I figured I'd have to go farther than that with you, old man," Dance said softly. "I figure I'll have to drive you and your brood clean out of the country."

The seriousness of the threat seemed to stun Christian Slate for a minute, then he laughed and got out of his chair. "All right, Dance, you come on. I'll be here, and I'll meet you. But remember, when I kill you, it's nothin' personal, just somethin' that I have to do." He waved his hand at the porch. "The talk's over. Sit until your wife comes. But don't come back, either of you. She picked her side."

5

The visit lasted longer than Shaw Dance wanted it to last, and by the time he drove into his own yard and got down, it was dusk.

"I'll put up the horses," he said and started to move away, but she took his sleeve.

"Thank you, Shaw. It's not easy for her to be alone now."

"It's all right," he said and led the team to the lean-to. He unharnessed them and turned them into a small corral, wheeled the buggy to the side of the barn, then washed in the trough.

Noreen was in the house, lighting the lamps; she would be getting supper in a minute. Dance sat down on the stone curbing of the trough and considered their situation. Living in that cabin had been no joy to her, he knew, for he had been petulant and uncommunicative, ignoring her when he could. It made him a little ashamed of himself, for she kept his place neat, cooked the best meals he had ever eaten, and washed his clothes; she was more of a wife than any man had a right to, he guessed, but they shared no common bed, and that made them strangers.

It was he who maintained the distance between them, he who did not offer her his smile, or let her know in any way that he did not wholly blame her for this wedded bond; in order to wring satisfaction from his feelings, he had to believe that she had wanted the marriage, for he felt a strong need to be the more deeply offended party.

The fact that he could think more philosophically about this, was, he supposed just getting used to having her around. All the more reason, he decided, to watch himself for she was young and pretty and any man alone would think about her.

Too much of that would lead him into trouble.

She called him to supper and he went across the yard and into the house. The table was set and she sat down as he slid his chair back. As he filled his plate, Dance said, "You're a good cook, Noreen." He glanced at her briefly. "Been meaning to tell you that, but somehow the words wouldn't come out."

"I know. You thought I'd read something into them that wasn't there."

Her accuracy surprised him. "Yes, that's it exactly." He laughed as though her observation had relieved him, and his manner visibly relaxed. "We got off to a real bad start, Noreen. There's no reason we can't part friends?"

It surprised him, the way her head came up, quick, and it fostered a gnaw of worry too. "Part?" she said.

"Well, we both know we can't go on like this," Dance said. "I'd be less than honest with you if I didn't say that Jane Meer and I have an understanding, sort of."

"I see," she said and went on eating, slowly.

"No, you don't really see," he said. "I talked to Harler, the lawyer, and he tells me we could get this marriage annulled."

"I don't know what that is," she said.

"It's a paper saying that we were never married at all," Dance said. "You just couldn't want to go on living this way."

"I could," she said firmly. "You've been good to me, Shaw."

"Naw, I haven't either. Why I've hardly been civil to you."

She shook her head. "You've been good to me, Shaw. I know you think about me, or why else would you have taken me home today. Am I pretty, Shaw?"

"Yes," he said. "I always thought that."

"Then if pa hadn't forced you the way he did, could you have ever looked at me like I was your sweetheart?"

"I don't know," Dance said. "What does it matter now?"

"It matters to me," she said. "It matters because no one's really loved me, not the way a woman wants to be loved."

He cleared his throat. "That kind of talk won't get us anywhere."

She reached out and touched his hand. "Shaw, do you have to stay in the barn? Does it help you keep from touching me?" She suddenly abandoned her place at the table and stood with her back to him. "I can't stand another night alone. I just can't!"

He remained silent for a time, thinking about this. "Noreen, it ain't right."

"Who says it ain't, anyway? I got the name, so I'm entitled to the game." She turned and looked at him. "Do you think your woman doctor believes we've never touched each other? Answer me straight."

Dance sighed. "I guess she thinks as most others seem to."

"You see what I mean? It's not right."

He nodded in agreement. "But there's very little right anyway. I've been hurt plenty. This little more won't kill me, or you either. One of these days, I'll drive you to town, put you on a train, and you can go to San Francisco and live like a lady. The lawyer can take care of all the papers and see that you have enough money to live in fine style, until you get a man who's right for you. And I wouldn't tell him about me, Noreen. He wouldn't understand. Nobody would."

"Suppose I told you I didn't want to go to San Francisco?" She met his amazed stare. "Suppose I said that you were right for me, and that's all I wanted?"

"I don't love you," Dance said.

"You don't hate me either," she said. "Shaw, I know you'll send me away sometime. I know it and I'm not fighting that. But I want to go with more than a valise, Shaw. Do you know what I mean?"

"No, not exactly."

"I want to be carrying your child."

He blew out a slow breath. "And prove your old man right?"

"He can count," she said. "You'd prove him wrong. But I don't want to prove anything. I just want to go with more than I ever had." She hesitated, then came over to him and put her arms around him, bending toward him to do so. "Would it be so difficult for you, Shaw? Would it be so hard to pretend?" He didn't brush her arms away, and this encouraged her; she put her lips to his. The warmth of her kiss ate slowly at his resistance, and he put his arms tightly about her and drew her onto his lap. They sat that way for a time. Then she got up and slid the bar on the door and turned to him and looked at him.

"We're all alone on a mountain, Shaw. It's kind of a good feeling, when you don't think about anything else."

Roe Carlyle worked late in his office, then he went to town and stepped inside Hanley's saloon for a drink. He saw Marshal Cove Butler at one of the tables, talking to Westbrook Arnold, the railroad man, and Carlyle remained at the bar until Butler got up and left.

Then he turned and approached the table before Arnold could leave.

"I'd like to buy you a drink," Carlyle said, taking Butler's warmed chair.

Arnold shrugged and Carlyle wiggled his finger. He said no more until the drinks had been served, then he rested his elbows on the table. "It was a smart move, Christian Slate marrying off his only daughter to Shaw Dance. Even a man like Dance will

113

hesitate now before declaring war."

"I can't see that," Arnold said.

Carlyle grinned. "The Slate girl's somewhat a beauty. Small, shapely. When a man beds down with a woman like that, he don't put her aside too quickly. I guess she's carrying too. The old man thinks so."

"You seem," Arnold said frankly, "to know what goes on behind every curtain in town."

Carlyle flushed, but he kept his temper in check. "My conclusion isn't far wrong. Dance met her mother at the hotel, and then took the girl home for a visit. Tonight I saw a light in his place on the mountain, so there was no trouble at Slate's. From that I conclude that there's been some kind of peace made."

"If I were paying for information," Arnold said, "I'd give you all of fifty cents for that. What's your point, Mr. Carlyle?"

"Just this. I think you'll wait a long time before Shaw Dance puts the old man on his knees and forces a sale to the right of way."

"So?"

"So back a different horse. Back me. Mining is the biggest interest around here."

"But not as permanent as cattle or timber," Arnold said. "Mr. Carlyle, every railroad west of the Mississippi has lost money."

"Then why build this spur line?"

"Oh, we'll make money on this, and in a small way, cut down the operating debt of the other lines. What can you offer?"

"Trouble for Christian Slate."

"How much?"

"Enough to make him lose money." He spoke softly. "Mr. Arnold, if things get so tough in town that Slate's men have no place to go, they'll pull stakes and leave. He can't run his place without a crew of sixty men." He smiled. "If I passed the word around that there would be a bonus in the pay envelope of every man who whipped a Slate rider, he'd be out of business in sixty days."

"That would cost you considerable money," Arnold pointed out.

"Not if the railroad split the cost," Carlyle said.

Westbrook Arnold thought about this, then smiled. "And what do you want out of it? Lower rates?"

"Shaw Dance," Carlyle said. "I want to play the game with him on his mountain, but I want to make sure I can keep what I win. With Slate in power, I don't think I could. Bucher doesn't worry me; I'd boot him off without raising a sweat. But once I get that mountain, I want to keep it."

"There must be a lot of gold there," Arnold said dryly.

"Not a lot, but there's a man there whose guts I hate."

"I can understand that. Suppose we drink to it and talk about when we can get started."

Christian Slate ate his evening meal alone in the big dining room; this was his way, to live like a feudal lord while his sons ate in the cook shack and his wife had her supper served to her in her room.

After his cigar, he went up the stairs to the big hall and knocked on his wife's door, then went in without waiting for her invitation; this was also his way, to always announce his coming, yet let everyone know that they were powerless to stop him.

She was sitting in a big chair, reading. Christian Slate said, "I guess you had a good visit, Maud."

"Dance is a good man," she said. "I told him I was lonely and he done something about it." She looked at Slate. "I want him to bring her back again, Christian."

"My word to him was not to come back."

"Change it."

"I can't do that," he said.

"Why? Because you've never changed

116

your mind about anything, even when you're wrong." She shook her head. "Christian, you may be big thunder elsewhere, but in this house you're just a man I once saw thirty years ago put his bare bottom on a rock and cry because he was too poor to buy a new pair of pants. But those were good days, Christian. You was just a man then, and a likable one."

"Ain't you ever going to forget that?" he asked. "The only time in my life when I ever broke down and you got to remember it."

"I guess it was the only time I ever saw the man in you, not the machine burning with ambition." She smiled. "Christian, I want my daughter to come visit me. She'll be carryin' one of these days and I want to see her now and then."

"She's carryin' now," Slate said.

"No, she ain't. You were wrong there, but like all the other times you were wrong, you ain't man enough to face up to it." She hunched her chair around to face him. "The wrong you did to that girl and Dance I'm never going to forgive you for, Christian. It was a mean thing to do. Now she's coming here when she pleases, or I'm going to her to stay."

He studied her beneath the thicket of his brows. "That's a bluff."

"Is it?"

"A word from me and not a man would dare drive you off the ranch."

"One man would. Shaw Dance."

Christian Slate laughed. "How would you get word to him?"

"I won't have to," she said. "My daughter knows she's to see me in a month. We talked of it when she was here. If she don't get to see me, Dance is to come for me."

"He won't," Christian Slate said. "Why should he?"

"Because there's man in him that you're blind to," she said. "Because when he was eleven his pony pitched him and I found him stretched out beside the road, a lump on his head the size of an egg. I took him home and gave him a glass of milk and some cookies I'd baked."

"I remember that," Christian Slate said.

"He remembers it too, Christian. How you come into the kitchen demanding to know how come that bastard was in your house."

Slate shook his head. "He's forgot that."

"No, he ain't forgot it. He remembers and he'll come for me because he's a good man, better than the one I married or the sons I raised."

This angered the old man and he pounded

118

his fist on the table. "This good man killed your son!"

"He shot him," Maud Slate said to correct him. "I lay the blame on you, Christian, because you taught them that greed was a right any Slate could enjoy." She pointed her finger at him. "When the day comes that you can speak out and admit that the only reason you hate Shaw Dance is because you see in him a better man than yourself, you'll find that you don't hate him anymore and can live in peace with yourself."

"Old woman, you've been alone in this room too long. With my dying breath I wouldn't utter such a thing."

"Then you're headed straight for hell for sure." She picked up some sewing and began working on it. "From my window I saw Morey riding out, leading a pack horse."

"He's going to Virginia City," Christian Slate said. "That ought to make you happy; he's deserting his family."

She shook her head. "No, I don't fool myself that way. Morey knows he'll follow Frank to the grave; he never had good judgment, or Frank's nerve. I won't think that he's ashamed of his name; he's too much a fool for that. He only thinks of his skin."

"You have a poor opinion of your sons."

"I know my sons," she said. "He'll come back, Christian, when it's safe. But he would never fight Shaw Dance, yet he was afraid he would have to. Does that hurt your pride, Christian, to know there's a touch of coward in the Slate blood?"

"If there is, he inherited it from you," he said and slammed out of the room.

6

Shaw Dance hated to admit it, but he liked Max Bucher for a partner; they spent weeks together, cruising the timber on the flanks of the mountain, camping together where nightfall caught them, and they talked, not much at first, but more as their association grew into a solid friendship.

There was, on Bucher's part, a deep, genuine respect for Shaw Dance; the man was more than a fighter, a tough man who could stand for himself. Dance had a sound head when it came to business, and, when he spoke of something, it was worth listening to. And Dance formed his opinion of Bucher, and had to change a few old ones to do it. He had always thought Bucher pretty much of a coward, but right after the saw camp had been set up, one of the governors on the steam engine went wild and a saw started to scream, picking up revolutions, threatening to explode and shower death around at any second. The operator, in his haste to get away, caught his pants cuff on the carriage roller and was pinned there. Bucher, knowing well how horribly he would die when that saw let go, ran in, calmly opened his pocket knife and cut that man free while Dance stood there with cold sweat on his face. Someone ran to the boiler and blew off the head of steam and the saw's howl died, but the risks were all there and Bucher had accepted them without batting an eye. Afterward they went over to the small office building and Bucher had a drink of whiskey. Then Dance knew that he really liked this man.

He said, "Max, if I ever hear anyone call you a fat German again, I'll knock his block off."

Bucher shook his head. "I'm fat and I'm German. What do I care?"

He waved his hand. "Shaw, I live for myself, not for them —" He motioned toward the town. "I know you care, but I don't. Let them think of Max Bucher as a fat German. Inside, I know what kind of man I am, and it satisfies me." He offered the bottle to Dance, and, when he declined, he put it in his desk drawer. "Let's get back to work now."

He was, Dance discovered, a working man; Bucher liked to be doing, and he wasn't one to waste his time. They spent nine days on the west flank of the mountain, marking out a future road and blazing trees to be cut. He learned then that Bucher wasn't a glutton; he didn't want to denude the mountain of timber, but picked only the big trees to fall, leaving thick stands to grow, and in this way insured himself of cutting for the next forty years.

They had worked their way into the highest reaches and in midafternoon Dance said, "Why don't we spend the night at my place?" He pointed toward the rising pinnacles of rock. "I know a foot trail that will get us through by dark."

Bucher grinned. "Nine days away is a long time."

"It ain't that at all," Dance said and started walking.

The climb was slow in spots and dangerous, for there were times when the footpath clung to sheer walls and they had no more than an eight-inch clef to cling to.

By the time the sun was down they broke out just above Dance's mine and walked on down to the clearing. Noreen was in the yard loading firewood into a basket, and, when she saw Dance, she smiled and waved.

Bucher made a wry comment. "Well, something has changed anyway." Dance gave him a quick glance and it seemed to Bucher that a quick rush of blood came to the man's face, but in the waning light he couldn't be sure.

Dance carried the wood inside the house for his wife then came out and joined Bucher at the spring. He handed the German soap and towel, then splashed water over his face.

As Bucher dried, he said, "I couldn't help but notice that your things are gone from the barn." He paused a moment before saying more. "It was bound to be, Shaw."

"It's not a good thing," Dance said softly. "But it was more than I could fight."

"A fool would have gone on fighting it," Bucher said. "She's a good woman, Shaw. In time —"

"— she's liable to hate me," Dance said quickly. "She knows I don't love her, Max. I wish I did. I wish I could change that. Maybe it's her accepting things the way they are that bothers me. It just started out bad and it'll end bad."

"It's the way you look at most things," Bucher said. "Sometimes it's not that way at all, Shaw."

"I never asked for much," Dance said. "Just respect, what was due me."

"You miss the whole point," Bucher said. "Shaw, the way people are, the way they think, you didn't have much coming. Sure it wasn't your fault your pa and ma never got married. It wasn't your fault you were born. And it ain't your fault because people got big mouths and like to talk about other people. But you fought for your respect all right, and wound up with more people afraid of you than respecting you." Bucher folded the towel. "This woman is good for you, Shaw. Give her a chance."

"I can't forget the way I was made to marry her."

"You've got to forget that," Bucher said. "You've got to forget all the meanness that was ever done to you, because no matter how much you hit back, you'll never really even it all up."

Noreen came to the door. "I've got supper on, and I'm lonesome for talk."

They went into the house, Bucher first, and, when Shaw Dance came in, Noreen reached out and took his hand and Dance quickly pulled away before Bucher turned his head and saw that. He was instantly sorry because a deep hurt came into her eyes, then she went to the stove and turned her back to him and he sat down at the table to consider his stupidity.

Dance said nothing for a moment, then he slapped the table and got up and went over to her and took the big spoon from her hand and turned her so she faced him squarely. "A minute ago," he said, "I done something that was wrong."

"I don't want to talk about it," she said, and tried to free herself from his grip.

"But I do," he said. Bucher was looking at them and he didn't care. "When I came in the door you touched me and I pulled away like I didn't want Bucher to know I'd ever touched you before. I've got to stop pretending, Noreen. Do you know?"

"Shaw, what's between us is between us and —"

"I don't live two lives," Dance said. "Neither do you." He put his arms quickly about her and kissed her and held her that way for a long moment, then he released her. "Now that's what I should have done and I'm sorry I didn't the minute I saw you."

She seemed on the edge of tears, then she threw her arms around his neck and gave him a brief, intense hug, then turned to her cooking, as though she was embarrassed. Dance raised his hand and brushed a strand of hair from her face and she smiled, pleased beyond her words to say.

Bucher cleared his throat. "I like you now, Shaw. This was the part that was missing, but it ain't now. It'll work out." He brought out his pipe, then hesitated. "Mind if I smoke, Mrs. Dance?"

"No, I don't mind." Then she looked at him. "It's the first time anyone ever called me that. I like it."

"I was happily married once," Bucher said. "Sit down, Shaw. She was a Dutch dumpling, but I loved her, my Helga. The fever took her and three children when she was twenty-nine. A man sort of loses his soul after that."

"I didn't know that, Max."

"People have troubles of their own," Bucher said. "They don't want to hear mine." He looked at Noreen and smiled. "One of these days soon, your husband is going to be a rich man. You could go to San Francisco and live in a big house and ride in a fine carriage."

"I can do for myself," she said, bringing a filled platter to the table. "Mr. Bucher, I've spent my life in a big house filled with men. Money wouldn't buy me anything I don't have right now. I'm free, Mr. Bucher. I don't have to lock a door to make sure I'm not disturbed. And I can listen all day without hearing a man swearing. If Shaw makes a lot of money, then I'm glad for him, but it doesn't matter to me."

"There's nothing left for me but the money," Bucher said. "It's too bad, but I can't change it. Life's just a series of bargains we make with ourselves, and like any other bargain, it's only good as long as you stick to it."

They ate and talked about the logging, and while Noreen washed the dishes, Dance and Bucher went to the porch to smoke. They had hardly half finished their cigars when a horseman rode slowly up the pass and Dance got up and reached inside the door for his rifle.

Then the rider paused and Cove Butler called out: "Shaw? I want to come in."

"Come on then," Dance said and leaned his rifle against the wall. Butler rode on to the clearing and dismounted, but left the reins dropped.

"Are we friends, Shaw?"

"As good as I'll ever have, I guess," Dance said. "What's wrong?"

"Trouble," Butler said. Noreen came to the door and stood framed in the light and Butler immediately tipped his hat. "Evenin'," he said, then spoke to Dance. "I can't put my finger on it, Shaw. It started around five o'clock. Slate paid today and a gaggle of his riders came to town."

"That's usual," Bucher said.

"That's so," Butler said. "But Roe Carlyle paid today too."

Bucher grunted softly. "Changed it? Wonder what for."

"I don't know that either," Butler said. "But the saloons are filling up with more men than I can handle. Already a couple of Slate's men have been pushed around on the street. There wasn't any trouble, but only because the foreman was there and stopped it. Shaw, will you come back to town with me?"

"I'll get my coat," Dance said.

The caution in Bucher made him put out his hand. "This isn't your fight, Shaw."

"It is, 'cause he asked me," Dance said and got his coat and hat. When he stepped out to the porch he picked up the rifle, held it for a moment, then replaced it against the wall.

Bucher said, "You're changing, Shaw. Getting considerate. Watch out. When Christian Slate hears of it, he'll push against you."

"I'll push back," Dance said and got his horse.

He rode out with Butler and Dance led

the way down for Butler was none too familiar with the trail. There was no talk while they traveled the bad part, but, when they hit the new stretch of road, Butler sided Dance. "I didn't ask anyone in town to help me," Butler said. "I knew what they'd say, that I was being paid to do the job, so do it."

"You don't have to explain it," Dance said. "They ought to give you a deputy."

"Not with Roe Carlyle on the board," Butler said.

When they came to the main street, Dance could see what had alarmed Butler; the streets were packed with moving men, miners and cattlemen, and the two weren't mixing well. The miners were crowding and walking up and down four abreast and the cowboys were riding their horses up and down, parading the superiority of the mounted man over the one afoot.

Butler and Dance worked their way through to the jail and went inside and closed the door, but walls did not completely shut out the sound, the bee-buzz babble of so many men talking and calling and moving; it reminded Dance of some undecipherable foreign tongue.

"It's going to blow up," Butler said. "I can hear the fuse burning."

"There has to be a reason," Dance said. "Have you talked to Carlyle?"

"No time," Butler said. "I rode for you as soon as I was sure." He went to his desk and opened a drawer and took out a pistol in a holster. "You'll need this."

Dance shook his head. "Let me have a chair rung or a sawed off billiard cue. A man who'd carry a gun in that mob is liable to get killed with it."

Butler rummaged through another drawer, talking as he searched. "A salesman came through six months ago. Left me a couple of — ah, here they are." He tossed two shot-filled leather saps on the desk. "The Chicago police are using them. The salesman tells me you can put a man to sleep with these and never break the skin."

Dance picked one up, slipped the loop over his wrist and hefted it a couple of times. The flexibility of the handle pleased him, and he dropped it in his pocket. "This will do fine. Be a good idea if you left your Colt here and took the other one." He went to the window and looked out, studying the traffic. "Roe's always been careful not to pay during the week Slate pays. It was the best way in the world to keep the biggest share of each outfit out of town at the same time. Now he changes all that. Why?" He turned and looked at Butler. "Roe Carlyle plays strange and silent games. I'd like to know the rules he uses."

"He's playing it against the Slates, obviously," Butler said. "Shaw, would you walk over to Judge Heckett's house and be deputized properly? A badge on your shirt will be a help out there." He nodded toward the street.

"All right," Dance said and turned to the door.

They stepped out and he waited while Butler closed the door, then both men turned their heads toward the center of town. There was a sudden surge to the hum, a deeper, more penetrating throbbing to the life on the main street, then a man shouted and it was lost in the yelling.

Butler said, "It's started," and began to run.

Dance followed at his heels and they headed for the packed mob in the street, rudely ramming their way through. A burly miner tried to block Dance and he swung the blackjack, felling the man like a tree. He knocked two more down before he got through to the center of it where fifteen miners fought with eight Slate riders. He took the first man he could reach and dropped him, trying all the time to stay near

131

Butler, to cover the man's back.

And he wasn't sure at all if he could do this, or cover his own.

7

The fight was simply a swirl around Shaw Dance. He could make out few distinct details, and had he quit it at that moment and been asked later who had participated in it, he would have been unable to name a single man. Yet there was something clear to him, an impression, a feeling he got in those furious moments, a feeling that there was no rage here, except the anger of the Slate men for having been picked on. Dance saw a miner's eyes, and there was no anger there, just the grim purpose of a man doing a job.

How he stood on his feet, Dance couldn't say; he was jostled and hit and knocked down once, but he got up and with Butler's help, managed to stop the fighting. Seven men were stretched out in the street and the others stood there, sullen and bleeding.

"All right," Butler said. "Get on down the street to jail!"

He put it out hard and quick, in a way he had, and, before they could think about it, they started moving. Then it was too late to change for he had them and they knew it. As he brushed past Dance, he said, "Have the others carried to the jail."

A motion of his hand brought the help he needed from the onlookers and the unconscious men were carried rudely down the street. When they were laid on the jail floor, Dance ushered the helpers outside and closed the door. Butler was locking the cell blocks and he came into the office. There was a welt on the side of his face, but no other mark. He smiled and tossed a ring of keys on his desk.

"There's a pair of fire buckets outside the door," he said. "Throw the contents on them and see if we can't get them on their feet."

Dance got the buckets and threw water on them and they began to stir and sit up and rub their heads. One of the Slate riders was first on his feet and he had to look around twice before he realized where he was.

"Am I arrested?" he asked.

"No," Butler said. "What's your name?"

"Harvey."

"Is your foreman in town, Harvey?"

"Which one? We got five."

"Any of 'em," Butler said.

Harvey continued to rub his head. "I

guess Childs is. I saw his horse on the street."

"Fetch him," Butler said. "Then go get yourself a drink."

The rider went out and Butler had the others sit on the floor; the cowboys moved to one wall and the miners pulled into a clannish knot. Butler looked at them until they grew nervous, then he asked, "Who started this?"

One of the miners said, "I don't like to be pushed on the street."

"If you say we pushed you," a Slate man said, "then you're a liar."

They all seemed to get to their feet at the same time, and Butler took his revolver from the desk drawer and cocked it. "I'm going to shoot the foot off the first man who closes. Now sit down and keep quiet and we'll get to the bottom of this." He pointed to one of the miners. "You go get Roe Carlyle and tell him to get over here."

"Can I go then?"

"I know you by sight, if I want you for anything."

The man left and Butler sat down behind his desk and rubbed the back of his neck. Then he took a bottle of whiskey from the bottom drawer and tossed it to one of Slate's men. With a grin of thanks, the man uncorked it and drank, then passed it to the man next to him. There wasn't much left by the time it reached the miners and they grumbled about it, but fell silent when Butler turned his head and looked at them.

One of the Slate riders said, "What brought you in on this, Dance?"

"Butler asked me," Dance said.

The door opened and Pete Childs came in. He was a tall, bony man in his midforties and he had seen enough trouble in his life so that very little really bothered him. He nodded curtly to Dance and said, "Slate men been acting up, marshal?"

"Where were you when the fight took place?"

Childs smiled. "Enjoying a lady's company. You married men might not understand that." His smiled faded. "You want me to pay some fines or something?"

"I want to find out how a fight started," Butler said. "Childs, did Christian Slate give you orders to make trouble?"

"He's got enough trouble of his own without coming to town to hunt for it," Pete Childs said. "These boys ain't from my section, but I'll do what I can. No, sir, the old man didn't order no trouble made. He's got range dryin' up in spots and water holes goin' muddy, and wolves after the calves, and enough to keep ten men worried sick."

The door slammed open and young Leed Slate paused there. He looked at Childs and at the Slate men, still squatted by the wall, and he said, "Get to your feet."

"They're all right where they are," Butler said evenly. "Close the door, Leed. Bugs come in after the light." He waited patiently and then Leed heeled the door closed. "I suppose you just got to town?"

"That's right," Leed Slate said. He looked at Shaw Dance. "I don't have to ask what side you was on, do I?"

"No, don't waste your time," Dance said.

"When you're in here," Butler said, "peg your gun belt."

Leed looked at him a moment, then laughed, and Shaw Dance said, "Do it and behave yourself."

Turning on him, Leed said, "I've been waiting for you to say something like that to me." He swung and Dance blocked him, then brought the blackjack down, catching Leed along the base of the neck. Dance expected results, but not what he got; Leed slumped and went to his knees, his right arm hanging numb and useless.

"Take his pistols," Butler said. "You look like a cool man, Childs. I'll let you hang 'em up."

A buggy, hastily driven, struck a wheel against the hitching post in front of the jail, then Roe Carlyle came in, obviously angry at being summoned so shortly. He looked around briefly and seemed unimpressed.

"What do you want of me, Butler?"

"Shifting your damned payday has made a mess," Butler said. "You'd better do something about it, Roe."

Carlyle's expression was fixed and stubborn. "I run my own business." He saw the bruises on the faces. "A little fight?"

"You know there was a fight," Dance said. "Maybe you wanted it that way."

Carlyle looked at him. "Can I help it if they fight. Hell, if it's too tough for the Slates, let them stay out of town."

Leed Slate said, "Carlyle, if you want trouble, the Slates can give you all you can handle."

"That remains to be seen," Carlyle snapped.

"All right, Roe, you're playing one of your little games. Leed, get your men out of here. There'll be no charges or fines. Tell your father I'll ride out and see him in the morning."

"Can I have my shootin' irons back? If it's all right with Mr. Dance."

Butler nodded and the Slate faction went

137

outside. Carlyle said, "What about my men?"

"They started it, so it won't hurt them to hear what the judge has to say."

"He may have more to say than you think," Carlyle said flatly. "I'm going to get him out of bed right now."

"Your privilege," Butler said and listened to the door slam. "He wants trouble. Willing to pay for it too." He rubbed his chin. "I can't see what he hopes to gain."

"Pete Childs gave you a hint without thinking," Dance said. "Take a mind's eye look at the Slate holdings. It's a day's ride on a fast horse from the southern reaches of it to the main house, and a three-hour ride from the town road to the house. Extending east, he must have seventy thousand acres; I hear his property reaches into the next county. That's a lot of land, a lot of problems for a man to have. You add them all up and he can't spare the time for trouble."

"He always found time to feud with you."

Shaw Dance shook his head and smiled. "Well, I'm just one man and it was sort of a hobby with Christian Slate. The kind of trouble Carlyle's got up his sleeve is different. Cove, I'd look for a brawl every time the two factions meet. It's in the cards. And if Roe's men can make it tough enough, the Slate men might not come to town."

There was a brightening in Butler's eyes; he said, "I think you've hit it, Shaw. If the Slate men get shut out, they'll quit the old man, leave him short-handed." He took out a cigar and lit it. "Someone's made a deal with the railroad."

"Yeah, and Roe likes to make deals." He stood up and pushed his hands into his coat pockets. "If you don't need me anymore, I think I'll take a walk." He put his hand on the knob and smiled. "Don't wait up for me."

Butler said, "Use good sense, Shaw. You've got a wife."

"You don't have to remind me," Dance said and went out.

He walked along and turned at the side street and climbed the steep road to Jane Meer's house. There was a lamp on in the hall, turned down, and the rest of the house was dark. Dance knocked and waited for her to open the door. He could see her outline through the frosted glass, and she asked, "Who's there?"

"Shaw Dance."

She slid the bolt back and he stepped inside. She had a robe pulled tightly about her. "What do you want, Shaw? It's late."

"I wanted to see you," he said. "Jane, I've thought about you."

"And I've tried not to think about you," she said. "Come into the kitchen. I'll put on some coffee." She turned from him and he reached out and caught her arm and kissed her, and, when he released her, she slapped his face.

"Comparing?" she snapped.

He could not answer her, for indeed he had been, and he was disappointed and hated to be disappointed. "I guess I've made a mistake," he said.

"No, I did," she said and raised her hand to his face. "I'm sorry because I wanted you to kiss me, Shaw. I wanted you to love me so I'd know I had a hold on you. That's selfish, but I've never been sure in my own mind just how much of a woman I really am." She smiled. "Let's have the coffee."

He went with her to the kitchen and took off his coat and sat down. While she measured the coffee and fired the stove, she said, "I hate her, Shaw. I've given up trying not to."

"The thing is done," he said. "Why talk about it?"

"Isn't that what you came here for, to talk?"

Dance shrugged. "Now that I'm here, I'm

140

not sure. Maybe I wanted to look at you, to prove that you were still more woman than I'd known before." He shook his head. "I guess I don't really know why I came here."

"Maybe I know," Jane Meer said. "You may be wondering what kind of bargain you got after all, whether it's better than you ever thought." She brought the coffee pot to the table and poured him a cup. "Shaw, you're the only man I ever met who didn't try to change me into something I'm not. That's because you're strong and sure of yourself and you don't have to twist a woman around to prove anything. I told you once that I wasn't sure that I could love you, but now I am. I don't want you to go back to her. Abandon her if you have to. What do you owe her anyway?"

She had, he realized, neatly boxed him, for she knew what course he would take, what course he had to take. Dance said, "As long as she's legally my wife, I'll stay with her. You don't want a man who'd do different."

"Do you have to go back tonight?" she asked.

He thought about this, trying to cut to her true meaning, or what he thought she meant. "Do you want me to stay?"

"Yes." She got up and came around and

sat on his lap, her arms around his neck. "I am the woman you thought me to be, Shaw. More than she is, or ever will be."

His mind was a millrace of contradiction, a part of him inclining toward her desire while another part rejected her for reasons of principle he never knew he had. He thought of Noreen, protected, innocent, and badly used by life. And he thought of Jane Meer, who possessed every advantage and who had the nerve to use it.

He was, he realized, about to do something that he would be ashamed of, and it was a shock to him for he could not recall ever having done anything shameful. He tried, gently, to ease her off his lap, then he ended by lifting her and standing himself.

"I guess it's too late for coffee," he said and turned to his coat.

He was not prepared for her fury; she threw the coffee pot at him, showering the wall. Then the fury hardened her face and her voice was strange to him.

"Oh, she must treat you real good, Shaw!"

There was no reason to answer her, to prolong this; he just wanted to get out where the night air was chilly. "I'm sorry," he said and started down the hall.

She followed him, hitting him on the back and shoulders with her fists. Before he opened the door she flung herself against it and faced him. "Shaw, if you leave me now, if you go back to her now, I'll see you in hell for it."

"They say I'll have company," Dance said and pushed her aside and stepped out. He didn't really breathe decently until he reached the street.

When he got back to the jail, he found Cove Butler and Judge Heckett talking. Butler said, "Come in, Shaw. Close the door. I was just telling his honor that we can't have fist fights in the street every Saturday night. They may be fist fights now, but when the Slate riders start banding together, it's going to turn into ax handles, then knives and guns."

Heckett cleared his throat. "It's touchy business, marshal, but then one must expect some friction between factions."

"A little, I expect," Butler said. "This is more than a little, judge, and you know it. Now I'm going to talk to Christian Slate, and if he'll go along with it, I want Carlyle's men, and all the Slate riders put under a peace bond."

"My, that's a little extreme," Heckett said.

Shaw Dance spoke softly. "It's no use, Cove. Can't you see that the money got to him?"

"I resent that!" Heckett snapped.

"Go ahead and resent it," Dance told him. "Who paid you? Carlyle, or the railroad?"

"I don't have to listen to this," Heckett said and, marched to the door. He pointed at both of them. "You'd do well, Dance, to keep out of the marshal's affairs. And Butler, don't make a tempest in a teapot. That's good advice to both of you."

After he slammed the door, Butler sighed and sat heavily in his chair. "Well, I know where I stand anyway. You might as well go home, Shaw. And thanks."

"You know my name," Dance said, smiling. "Holler again if you need me."

He paused on the street, then mounted his horse and rode through town. The main street was still dense with traffic, but there was no more sign of trouble and Dance figured that it was over for the night; Carlyle had probably only primed a handful of men to set this off so he could see how the reaction went.

The night was turning chilly and Dance turned up the collar of his coat and rode with his head down for there was a wind blowing. He left the lights and sounds of the town behind and rode slowly along the dark road, letting his mind run over events. He couldn't care much about Carlyle's plans; the man failed to arouse respect or loathing or much of anything in Shaw Dance. He supposed that he regarded Carlyle as a nothing, a man not worthy of consideration, and he wondered what made him feel like that for Carlyle had education and money and a good position with a big company.

He didn't want to compare Carlyle with Jane Meer, but there was a lot of similarity there. She was willing to use him for what she wanted and he didn't like that; she had been willing to judge harshly for by doing so, her judgment of herself was less severe.

Somehow his attraction toward her had dimmed, and this bothered him for he wasn't a man who changed much, and each change was a mild disturbance.

"Hold up!"

This was a shout, sudden, and threatening, and he reined in his horse. Leed Slate and Pete Childs appeared on either side of the road, and in the faint light Dance could see that Leed had a pistol in his hand.

"Do you want to shoot or talk?" Dance asked.

"The gun is to make sure we talk," Childs said softly. "Dance, you can understand that."

"I guess I can. All right, talk. I'm tired

and I want to go home."

"We'll let pa do the talking," Leed said.

Dance swore softly. "A ride to your place and back — hell, I won't get home before morning."

"You've stayed out late before," Leed said. "Let's go."

Dance had no choice, so he moved out and Pete Childs fell in a few paces behind and he remained that way until they reached the Slate ranch. The lights were on downstairs and Dance knew that the Slate riders had already told of the trouble in town. When they dismounted by the porch, Kyle came out, a bandage about his head.

He looked at Dance bluntly, then turned and led the way into the old man's parlor. Christian Slate wore a robe and slippers and he puffed on a cigar. Then he waved his hand and Dance sat down and Kyle brought glasses of whiskey to them.

"I regret that you came here at gunpoint," Christian Slate said. "I heard what went on in town. I heard of your part in it."

"Then why bring me here?"

"I want to know why," Slate said. "I want to know why you took the side of my men."

"My war's always been with you, old man. You and your sons." He tossed off his whiskey and put the glass aside. "Besides,

Cove Butler asked me to help him."

"What do you owe Butler?"

"The courtesy he's always extended to me," Dance said.

Christian Slate considered this, but Dance could see that he didn't believe it for it would never have been a reason to him. Finally Slate said, "What's Carlyle trying to do anyway? I never asked for trouble with him."

"He's trying to break you," Dance said. "In that, I applaud him. It's the way he does business that I detest."

"The fool! I don't break easy."

"He won't tangle with you," Dance pointed out. "It isn't his way. But he'll make it tough for you to keep men on the payroll, and you can't run this place without a crew. He's got six hundred men on his payroll. You've got how many? A hundred and ten or twenty? All of Carlyle's men can come to town at one time. Only half of yours can. In another week it won't be safe for a Slate rider to appear on the streets, day or night."

"My men aren't afraid of odds," Slate snapped.

"Sure, they're brave enough, but they won't do without tobacco or a drink of whiskey or a romp at Big Ella's place. They'll get disgusted and quit, and the word will get around and it'll be tough to hire more. So you'll have to pull in, sell off, tighten up."

Christian Slate stared at Shaw Dance. "How is it that you can tell me this? How do you know that's the way it will be?"

"Roe Carlyle is a thin man. I don't have much trouble seeing through a thin man." He started to get up but Leed put his hand on his gun.

"Pa's not through."

"Then he'd better get through. I want to go home."

"I hear that Butler's coming in the morning," Christian Slate said. Shaw Dance nodded and the old man pulled at his mustache. "Then we'll wait until he gets here. I like to get the law's opinion before I ride on a man and wipe him out."

This was unexpected and Shaw Dance did not bother to hide his surprise. "Slate, don't be a damned fool! Butler would never stand for that."

"We'll see," the old man said. "Have another drink. Leed, go see if your mother is awake. She'll likely want to hear about Mrs. Dance."

8

Without having it put into words, Shaw
Dance realized that he was a prisoner of
this powerful and narrow-minded old man.
He spent some time talking to Mrs. Slate,
then, when the dawn began to break, he
went downstairs and found Christian and
his sons still waiting. Kyle was sleeping in a
chair while Leed stood by the front door.

He said, "Daylight soon. Butler won't
waste time."

"I hope the man's reasonable," Christian
Slate said. He turned his head and found
Shaw Dance watching him. "No man has
ever raised his hand against me and got
away with it. I can't make an exception in
Roe Carlyle's case. Butler either stands
aside, or I'll put him aside."

"You can't do that," Dance said softly.
"Old man, we've been enemies for years;
that must count for something. At least we
have some respect for each other because
I've never licked you and you've never
licked me."

"You've stood up to me," Slate said. "I'll
admit that. Have your say then."

"No one has to tell you about Butler. He'll
keep the peace and he's not afraid of you."

"Maybe he ought to be," Leed said.

"Keep quiet, boy," the old man chided. "Dance, I never make a man do what he don't want to do. I'll talk with Butler, then he can do what he feels he has to do. You can do the same."

Dance stood there for a moment, then he said, "You know that Butler will stand up to you. You know it and you're going to kill him."

"Butler's like I am," Christian Slate said. "He does what he has to do."

Shaw Dance knew what *he* had to do and wondered if he could. Kyle snored briefly and the old man sat there, head tipped forward while Leed stared out across the yard. There would be, Dance decided, no moment where their awareness was lower, and he moved, grabbed Leed, flung him around until the boy's body shielded him from the old man and Kyle.

Leed bawled out in surprise, but it was too late; Dance scooped one of the pistols from Leed's holster, slapped him across the head with the barrel and as the boy wilted, he fisted the other gun.

"Now just stay put," Dance said, cocking both pistols. Kyle stared sleepily but the old man didn't stir.

"You're just putting it off until another day," Christian Slate said.

"That's what I'll do then," Dance said. "Cove Butler doesn't die this morning."

"Then some other morning," Slate said. "Relax, son. Go look to your brother."

Kicking open the door, Dance backed out, took the first horse he came to and went into the saddle with one flip. He rode out of the yard as fast as the horse could go and didn't look back.

A mile from the house he slowed and found that no one was after him, yet he was on Slate land and he wasn't safe. He followed the town road as the sky grew lighter, and finally a peep of sun showed. He rode with one pistol thrust into his belt and the other in his hand, and ahead he saw a rider approaching and recognized Cove Butler's sorrel.

They met and halted and sat facing each other. Butler said, "That's a pretty pair of six-shooters, Shaw. If I didn't know better I'd swear that Leed Slate owned a pair just like that."

"He did," Dance said. "There's no use going any farther, Cove. The old man means to kill you."

"That's pretty drastic," Butler said. "Tell me about it." Dance did, and, when he was through, Butler lit a cigar. "Yes, I wouldn't stand for a war. All right, we'll have to think

151

of something else." He turned his horse and they rode together. "You took a chance for me, Shaw. Thanks."

"I've been wondering about it," Dance said. "I did it pretty easy, as though it had been set up for me. Maybe the old man didn't really want to have this talk for fear it would go farther than he wanted it to. Maybe he was figuring that I'd stop it in time."

"You did," Butler said. "But it's only been put off until another day, Shaw. The old man will raise his army and ride on Carlyle."

"That's what he said, about this only being put off until some other time," Dance said. He shook his head. "I'd like to see the old man get his, but I'll be damned if I can make up my mind just how. For a lot of years I've held my hate for the Slates, but I'll tell you, Cove, it gets harder to keep going all the time."

Butler said, "For as long as I've known you, Shaw, you've been bent on vengeance, but you could never quite make up your mind as to what form it would take. But you and I both know that the Slates have suffered more at your hands than you have at theirs."

"Depends on how you look at it," Dance said.

"You know I'm right."

They parted at the fork of the road and Dance took the road up his mountain. As he passed the logging camp he saw Max Bucher and waved and kept on going, arriving at his cabin during the sun's first strong morning heat.

Noreen came to the door as he put up the horse, and she saw the Slate brand. When he came to the house, she said, "When you didn't come back, I — why are you riding that horse?"

He smiled and kissed her. "Long story and not very interesting. I may tell you the interesting parts while you cook some bacon and eggs."

She regarded him solemnly. "You've got a bruise on your face. But you're happy. What makes you happy, Shaw?"

"You do," he said. "Some day I must tell you about that too."

Westbrook Arnold sat in Roe Carlyle's office. The sun was down and the gray shadows of night were thickening, but neither made a move to light the lamp. Carlyle was at the telescope and he turned away finally, a trace of irritation in his manner.

"Butler came back too quick. From that I conclude that he never got to Slate's place."

Carlyle raked a match across the underside of his desk and put it to his cigar. "I hadn't counted on Dance being in this."

Westbrook Arnold laughed softly. "Carlyle, when the game is big, you've got to expect the unpredictable. That peace officer is a stronger force than I first thought. I don't suppose money . . ."

"You're out of your mind," Carlyle said quickly. "Butler and Dance go by their conscience. You would, I suppose, consider that an advantage, because we don't."

"We're not paid to fail," Arnold said softly. "Well, where do we stand? We don't know the old man's reaction because Butler never got there. Butler would, being in the middle, have come to you with terms for peace." He sighed and helped himself to one of Carlyle's cigars. "Suppose we try again next week?"

"I guess so," Carlyle said. "Only Butler will be looking for trouble this time."

"Naturally." Arnold sat in silence for a time, then leaned forward quickly. "Let me ask you a quick question and give me your answer equally fast before you can temper it with fear or good sense. Do we really need Butler?"

"No," Carlyle said, then fell silent.

"How can it be done?"

"I wouldn't want any suspicion to fall . . ."

"Naturally, naturally. How can it be done?"

Carlyle thought about it. "It would have to seem as though it were Christian Slate's work. A note? Something to tie this up in a neat package." He puffed on his cigar. "Where the road forks there's a . . ."

"I don't need to know the details," Arnold said. "Can you get someone to take care of it? Say, in a week?"

"Yes," Carlyle said. "Maybe before."

"Good," Arnold said, rising. "Let's go to the hotel for supper. We'll let the railroad pay for it."

The next day, Carlyle stayed in his office, taking care of some routine work and trying to figure out how he could successfully fabricate a message that would pass for Christian Slate's. Then it dawned on him that there might be a sample in the bank; Slate did business there, a lot of it, borrowing and paying back, and transferring money.

An excuse to go to the bank was always handy, and Carlyle timed it so that the president would be out and only a lone clerk would be in charge. The clerk was perfectly agreeable to Carlyle's suggestion that he wait in the president's office, and this gave Carlyle a chance to browse. Without being observed, he cracked a file or two, found a letter from Christian Slate, and pocketed it.

His first impulse was to leave, but that would invite comment; so he waited, and, when the president returned, Carlyle brought up some trivial matter, discussed it briefly, and went back to the office at the mine.

Behind the safety of a locked door, he read and reread the letter, and believed he could copy Slate's scrawl for there were many words he could use intact, including the signature. That evening he bought a cheap tablet from the foreman's shack and created a short, but entirely satisfactory forgery. Then he pocketed this, along with his revolver, and went to town.

Butler was not in his office and this gave Carlyle a chance to slip the note under the door and walk on down the street. He didn't want to go back to the mine and get his horse; someone might notice that it was gone. Renting one at the stable would be equally foolish, so he walked; it was only two miles, and he figured that he had plenty of time.

A dozen times he was forced to leave the road when riders passed, and finally he arrived at the junction. The road to the left veered sharply upward and began winding its way along the flank of Shaw Dance's mountain while the other road ran straight down the broadening valley floor.

The fork in the road was guarded on both sides by thick brush and Carlyle found a nest that gave him a commanding view, yet covered him completely. He considered his retreat and from this vantage point, could fade back, stay in the brush, and never be found. Once he was back in town he could return to the mine and claim he had fallen asleep in his office and no one in the world could doubt it.

Surprisingly, he was not nervous, or afraid; he took his revolver from his pocket and broke it open to check the cylinder and spilled three of the cartridges on the ground. Then he had to get down on his hands and knees and hunt for them and only succeeded in finding two. He had first thought of taking a rifle along, but that would have been too bulky; the .38 Smith & Wesson would do the job nicely enough, for the range would be point-blank, no more than fifteen yards.

Roe Carlyle settled down to wait with an infinite patience.

■ ■ ■ ■

In the early afternoon, Shaw Dance left
Max Bucher at the logging camp and rode
up the mountain to his own place. He
wheeled the buggy from the barn, hitched it
and brought it around to the door. Then he
got the large wooden tub, filled it from the
spring, and took a bath. Afterward he put
on his best clothes and said, "If you've got a
bonnet, put it on. I'm going to take you to
town."

She looked at him with a mixture of hap-
piness and surprise, then she said, "You
don't have to, Shaw. Really, it's all right."

He felt the color come into his face and
he knew what she meant, and he felt
ashamed for he had once swore to himself
that he would never appear in public with
her as his wife.

"I want to," he said. "Hurry up. I want to
get off the mountain by sundown."

"Well I've got to fix myself," she said and
began to hurry about. Dance laughed and
went outside to smoke and wait, and forty
minutes later she came out in her prettiest
dress.

"The night will be chilly," he said. "Better
bring a coat."

She had none, not a good one, so he went in and got one of his own and put it under the buggy seat. She wouldn't have to wear it in town where people could see it, but on the way home it would come in handy.

As they started down the mountain she held his arm and braced her other hand on the seat. "Why are we going to town, Shaw?"

"Oh, to have a good supper at the hotel. And maybe buy you a new dress or something nice." He laughed. "Or it could be we're going just to be going. I sometimes do things for no reason."

"I think no reason at all is sometimes the best reason."

Before they reached the bottom of the grade, Dance had to stop and put the heavy coat around her shoulders, for the chill was sharp and day's heat faded quickly after dark. They saw lights in Bucher's cabin and stopped on impulse and stayed an hour, then Bucher decided to ride into town with them; he got in the back of the buggy and Dance drove on down to the fork in the road.

There was a segment of moon rising, an orange light made so by a thin haze. Bucher said, "Snow before long. I'm glad we're moving timber off the low levels. Hate to shut down in the winter."

As they approached the fork in the road, Dance said, "Rider coming," and pulled up. Then Cove Butler came alongside the buggy and stopped.

"Hello, there," Butler said. He peered in back. "That you, Bucher? Kind of cramped, ain't it?"

"You look like a man with a purpose," Dance said. "Were you coming up to see me?"

"No," Butler said. "Going out to the Slates. Got a message from the old man to make peace talk. I guess Kyle or Leed dropped it off. I noticed both their horses tied up in front of Hanley's as I rode by."

"Where's your shotgun?" Bucher asked. "You'll need it to talk peace with Christian Slate."

"No gun at all," Butler said, opening his coat. "One of the conditions." He smiled. "The old man wouldn't shoot me cold turkey. Too much pride for that. Well —" He raised his hand briefly to the brim of his hat and started to ride on just as a pistol shattered the quiet.

Noreen yelled and started to fall from the buggy, but Bucher caught her, and the team, frightened by the sudden noise, bolted and they ran a hundred and fifty yards down the road before Dance could bring them to a halt.

Butler was yelling like a crazy man and driving his horse around in circles through the brush, then he gave it up and rode furiously to the buggy and flung off.

Bucher got down and struck a match while Dance supported Noreen on the seat. In the brief glare they could see that the bullet had taken her in the shoulder, not front and back, but crossways to the body.

"Give me your rifle," Butler said and Dance handed it over. "Take her into Doc Meer's. I'll see you later."

"That bullet was meant for you," Bucher said to Butler.

"Hell, I know that," Butler snapped and rode back to where the road forked.

"Hold her, Max, while I drive," Dance said and took the reins. He whipped the team into a run and tried not to hear his wife cry out as the rig jolted her. When he came onto the main street, he hardly slackened his pace at all and the few pedestrians that were crossing scattered like frightened chickens.

Dance wheeled up the side street and slid to a halt in front of Jane Meer's place, and Bucher handed her down to Dance who carried her to the door while the fat German ran on ahead and pounded to rouse the doctor.

Jane Meer was home, but she had just arrived for she still wore her coat and gloves. One look was all she needed. "Take her in there," she said, indicating her operating room.

Dance put Noreen on the table and took off her coat and threw it in one corner. She was bleeding badly and in pain, and Jane Meer unconcernedly cut away the shoulder of the dress and examined the wound.

"The shoulder is broken," she said, glancing at Shaw Dance. "Lover's quarrel."

"Don't be smart," he said flatly, and she stared at him for this was the tone he used in dealing with dangerous men; she had never heard it before. "Give her a shot or something to ease the pain."

"I'll have to give her ether," Jane said. "The quicker we get the bullet out, the better."

"Save it for me," Dance said. "I want to match it with the gun that fired it. And the man who pulled the trigger."

There was no more time for talk; Dance and Bucher stood aside while she placed a cone over Noreen's nose and dripped ether onto a cloth and a moment later her breathing grew steady and quiet.

Jane Meer worked with speed and efficiency; now and then she spoke. "I'd just come from the mine a few minutes before you arrived. An ore cart broke a man's foot and I'd just set it."

Butler came in and she only glanced at him; the lawman's expression was bleak. "No sign of the man who fired the shot. I stopped into Hanley's, but neither of the Slate boys had left the bar at any time. Shaw, I'm sorry. I'd rather have taken that bullet than her."

"I know that," Dance said.

Butler still carried Shaw Dance's rifle, and he took it. Butler said, "Don't make a mistake now."

"I'm going to make sure that I don't," Dance said. "Stay with her, Max. I'll be back." He stepped out and quietly closed the door, then walked rapidly through the house and out to the street.

Men saw him coming along the main street and got out of his way, and he pushed into Hanley's place and went straight to the bar. The men standing at the near side of Leed and Kyle Slate stepped back and Dance laid his rifle on the bar.

"We've been waiting for you," Kyle said.

"I'm here," Dance said. "Butler says you never left the place since you hit town. Who else says so?"

Hanley stood nearby. "I say so, Shaw. Is that good enough?"

"It satisfies me," Dance said, without looking at Hanley. "Kyle, that bullet was meant for Butler, but your sister got it instead. Your sister, and my wife. What are you going to do about it?"

"I've already sent for pa," Kyle said. He turned his head and looked at Shaw Dance. "I thought I'd wait and find out what *we* were going to do about it, Shaw. Let's find a quiet place to talk."

"Use my office if you like," Hanley said.

"Suits me," Kyle said and turned from the bar. They went to the rear of the building and down a short hall to Hanley's office. Leed closed the door and Kyle unbuckled his gunbelt and hung it on the clothes tree; after an initial hesitation, Leed did the same, and then Dance leaned his rifle against the wall.

Kyle said, "We were right, huh?"

"Right about what?" Dance asked.

"About you being the right man for her husband."

Dance opened his mouth as though he meant to deny this, then he said, "We've got along. But this is wasting time."

"It's about time we buried the hatchet," Kyle said. "Our trouble goes back a long ways, but it's been face-to-face trouble, Shaw. There's been nothing on either side that was sneaky. Now we've got a common anger. It would be foolish to go separate ways on it."

"Are you asking me to wipe everything out and —"

"I'm asking you to forget for awhile. Just like we're going to forget," Kyle said.

"The bastard who fired that shot is around somewhere while we're sitting here jawing," Leed said.

"Keep your mouth shut when men are talking," Kyle said. "We'll get to him, boy. You just keep your britches buttoned. Pa'll be here in another three hours. We'll wait and see what he wants to do. You can join us or go your own way, Shaw."

Dance thought it over, then said, "I'll wait too. Not that I think we'll do any better, but because I don't want you saying afterward that I wasn't big enough to give a little."

This made Kyle grin. "Shaw, you just can't back up an inch, can you?"

"Can you?"

"No, but it don't bother me like it does you." He got out his tobacco and made a cigaret. "How's Noreen?"

"Broken shoulder. I ought to get back to her now."

"You go ahead," Kyle said. "When pa gets here, Leed will come after you."

"All right," he said and went to the door, picking up his rifle on the way. "I'll never understand you people. All her life you ignore her, and now you're full of brotherly love."

"It's a man's world," Kyle said. "Not a very pretty one either, so a man shelters his women. They don't have to know about all the meanness that we do."

"They know about it," Dance said and left the back office.

As he passed through the saloon he saw Roe Carlyle sitting at a table and Carlyle put out his hand, touching Shaw Dance on the arm.

"I just heard. A terrible thing. Terrible." He seemed immeasurably sad. "If there's anything I can do —"

"Take your hand off my arm," Dance said. He raised the muzzle of the rifle and tucked it between Carlyle's chin and tie. "Now drink your beer and leave me alone."

Carlyle settled back in his chair, a hot anger brightening his eyes but in no other way changing his expression. "You've got no reason at all to treat me like this, Dance. I hold no ill feeling against you."

"Is that a fact?" Dance walked on out and

went down the street.

Butler had left Jane Meer's place by the time Dance got there; Jane was in the parlor, drinking a cup of coffee and she seemed very worn; her expression was drawn and she greeted Dance with no enthusiasm at all.

"She's resting now. I wouldn't bother her."

"I never have," Dance said.

She whirled on him, her temper high. "You like to pick apart everything I say, don't you?"

"It seems to be a common habit around here," Dance declared. "When can I take her home?"

"A week. Perhaps a bit longer. Ten days, say." She smiled thinly. "I hate to admit it, Shaw, but old man Slate was smarter than I gave him credit for. He married you off at gunpoint, but he knew the ingredients would mix." She finished her coffee and put the gun down. "It's a doctor's privilege to examine his patient, Shaw. I don't have to wonder anymore and you don't have to lie." Then bitterness came into her voice and she became hard-minded. "If there's a baby, call in another doctor. I won't deliver it."

"You just can't make up your mind what you want to be, a doctor or a woman, can you?"

"I can make up my mind," she said. "Now get out of here. I had a brutal two hours at the mine and the last hour and a half hasn't been easy. I need some sleep."

"Take good care of her," Dance said.

"You don't have to remind me of that, Shaw."

He left her place and walked toward Butler's office and found him in. The bullet taken from Noreen's shoulder was on the table, a badly battered piece of lead, and Butler was stirring it with the end of a pencil.

As Dance closed the door, Butler said, "I couldn't really tell what caliber it was until I took it down to Hanley's gold scale and weighed it. Thirty-eight without a doubt. Smith & Wesson more than likely. It's too light for a .38-40 or a .38 Colt." He threw the pencil aside. "If the shooter had used a rifle, Shaw, the bullet would have gone all the way through her and she'd be dead. If you were going to bushwhack a man, would you use a pistol?"

"I've always liked the rifle," Dance said. "It's not a good question to me for I'll take a rifle every time."

"Yes," Butler said, pulling at his lip. "Well, I carry a pistol all the time and a saddle gun when I'm traveling, but given a chance to draw a weapon, I reach for my .44 first and the rifle second. If I was going to waylay a man, I'd use a rifle. Especially at night. It would be steadier."

"Unless you had a good reason not to," Dance said. "Did you ever find where he had his horse hidden?"

"I don't think he was mounted," Butler said. "Figure out a few of the angles. If a man had a horse tied, there would only be one escape route, toward the horse. But if he was afoot, he could circle and duck about. Then too, the fork in the road is close enough to town so that a man afoot could get out and back."

"There's your reason for packing a six-shooter," Dance said. "The man we want would look conspicuous carrying a rifle, or even riding a horse."

"That sounds like a fair guess," Cove Butler said. "Oh, before I forget it. My wife says that Noreen can stay with her as soon as she's able to be moved. She told me to tell you that."

"I appreciate it," Dance said. He got up and stretched, then turned to the window. "Kyle wants me to bury the hatchet until we get to the bottom of this."

Butler smiled. "Well, that's some progress anyway. But let me direct your attention to a fact. The bullet was meant for me. I moved an instant before the shot was fired, and exposed your wife. Had I not moved, I'd have taken that slug in the ribs and it would have killed me, not quickly, but surely anyway. So someone wants me dead, and they'd have to stand to gain from it."

"You said you got a note from Christian Slate. Can I see it?"

Butler took it from his pocket and handed it over and Dance read:

Trouble I don't need. Come and talk. I'll carry no gun. You do the same.

C. Slate

"I've seen samples of his handwriting," Butler said. "He wrote that all right."

"Yes, it looks like his writing," Dance said, frowning. "But somehow it doesn't sound like him."

"What do you mean?"

"I can't really put my finger on it, Cove. The old man talks damned little, but as I can recall, he writes pretty formally. Let's take a walk."

"Where to?"

"Reilly's store. The old man has ordered a lot of stuff through Reilly, and maybe there's some letters in Reilly's file we can

170

look at." He and Butler stepped out. "It just doesn't ring true, Cove. Maybe I'm wrong."

"Maybe you're right too."

Reilly had some customers to wait on, so it was a few minutes before Butler could draw him aside.

"Do you have any letters or anything old man Slate may have written you, Reilly?"

The store keeper thought a moment. "I do have some. Come on back." He spoke to his clerk. "Mind the store, Herbie, and remember there's a sale on sugar. Eleven cents a pound. And watch how you sack it; my profit's narrow enough and —"

Butler took him by the arm. "We're in a bit of a hurry, Reilly."

"Oh, sure." He went into his back room where barrels and boxes crowded one another.

Butler said, "If you ever had a fire in here it would go up like a match."

Reilly's office was a roll-top desk crammed with papers and catalogues, and surprisingly enough, he seemed to know exactly where in the litter to dig. He produced two letters. "Got these last year when Slate ordered that metal watering trough and the fencing. I hope you find what you want. Excuse me. I've got to watch that boy. He simply can't read the scales right."

Butler backed around until lamplight fell on the paper. He read aloud. "Yours of the 15th instant at hand, and I beg to inform you —"

"That sounds more like the old man," Dance said. "He has a fair education and likes to rub it in. He sure has on me when I was a kid, pointing out that his sons would get it and I wouldn't."

After finishing the letters, Butler laid them amid the scatter of papers. "That doesn't mean the old man would write a note the same way."

"Yes, and it doesn't mean that he wouldn't. The chances are better that he would than wouldn't."

"Much better, I'd say." Butler stepped out of the cubbyhole. "Then it figures that he didn't write the note. Well, I really didn't think so myself an hour after the shot was fired. It's not the Slate way to pot a man. One thing, they've got their damned hog-sized pride and they never forget it. Look at the way Frank came after you, making his brag first so there'd be no mistake about it." He walked out through the store, thanked Reilly with a wave of the hand, then went on down to his office, neither man saying anything until the door was closed.

"I saw Roe Carlyle in the saloon tonight,"

Dance said.

Butler looked up quickly. "Funny you should mention him when I was just about to mention his name." Then he laughed and shook his head. "Nawwww, Roe doesn't have the guts to shoot a man."

"Face to face, maybe not," Dance said. "We don't know about the other."

"I'll have to find out where he was tonight," Butler said. "Shaw, this whole affair has changed my way of thinking. Would you help me again?"

"Whatever way I can."

"I'm a marked man. This time it didn't come off, but there may be another time, and, if it comes off, I want to leave a little law behind. Shaw, would you go over to Judge Heckett's with me and be sworn in as my deputy. We'll keep it quiet, but, if I get killed, I want the killer to find that he's bucking a man as tough as I am when it comes to enforcing the peace."

"Will Heckett do it?"

"Yes, because I've already talked to him."

They went out and across the town to Heckett's house and found the judge waiting. They exchanged a few words of pleasant conversation, then Heckett got out his record book and sat down at a table.

"If you have the badge, Mr. Butler, I'll

administer the oath. And Mr. Dance, I'd pin that to the inside of my coat until such time exposure to sunlight and public gaze is called for."

The oath wasn't much, Dance discovered, just his promise to abide by the Constitution, the laws of the State, and such judicial orders as issued. He swore to all this, pinned on the badge, and went back to Butler's office. Before they went in, Butler stopped.

"I've written up a will that I want you to witness, Shaw. Of course I'll leave everything to my wife. But I'd feel better if I knew someone was looking after her for awhile. No doubt she'll want to go back to San Francisco to her parents, so if you'll attend to the details —"

"You're not dead yet," Dance said.

"No, and I hope I won't be in the near future, but I'm not a fool; I like to keep my affairs straightened out as I go along. You're that way, so I won't have to explain it any further to you."

"All right," Dance said. He looked past Butler and saw Leed Slate coming down the street with a purposeful stride. As he drew near the jail, Leed saw them standing there and came up.

"Pa's over to the hotel now," Leed said. "He's ready to talk."

Butler said, "Is the law excluded from this?"

"Come over in a half hour," Leed said. "We'll be through with family business by then."

9

Christian Slate sat in a chair in the middle of the hotel room, and he faced the door. As soon as Leed and Shaw Dance stepped inside, Slate said, "Have you found out who fired the shot?"

"No," Dance said. He saw that the old man was heavily armed. "Don't you want to know how she is?"

"I know how she is," the old man said. "But alive or dead, I'd still want the man who fired the shot." He waved his hand. "Sit down, boy. Kyle, fetch Dance a chair." He waited until Dance sat down before speaking again. "You've been hard used at my hand, ain't you?"

"Everybody's been hard used at your hand," Dance pointed out. "But I suppose I've been used more than most."

"Can you forget that?" Christian Slate asked.

"I haven't any reason to," Dance said. "You've had your opinion for years. Likely it hasn't changed. Neither has mine."

"My daughter loves you, Dance. She wouldn't love a man unless he had worth."

Shaw Dance shook his head. "I've forgotten she's got Slate blood in her. She's not like the rest of you." He took out his tobacco and made a cigarette. "Is that what we're here to talk about?"

"No," Christian Slate said. "Like it or not, we've got something in common. She's your wife, and she's my daughter." He hesitated a moment, as though what he had to say wasn't easy. "You're my son-in-law, Dance. Kyle and Leed are your kin, by marriage."

"If you're going to ask me to call you papa, save your breath."

A quick anger came into the old man's eyes, then faded and he laughed. "Damn you, Dance, you're not afraid of me, are you?"

"Not a bit. Or of your tribe either."

"I've known that for years, but I'm just beginning to understand it. When I was a young man, I tried to be reasonable, but it didn't work. People mistook fairness for weakness, so I did what I had to do; I hit them with an iron fist and I hit them hard. There had to be only one way, the Slate way, and once I took a stand, I couldn't change it."

"Is that the way you have it figured?" Dance asked. "To me you've been a mean old man and there wasn't any excuse for it. I never liked the way you looked down on people. I still don't like it."

"Dance, we've got to stop fighting each other," Slate said. "As God as my witness, with my baby girl lying hurt, we've got to make peace."

"For how long?"

"For good," Christian Slate said. "Damn it, Dance, it hasn't been an easy compromise for me to make, but there's good blood in you. I guess the children you'll have will carry the best in both." He raised a gnarled hand and scrubbed it across his mustache. "I said some hard things at your wedding. I didn't mean them."

"A Slate always means what he says," Dance said. "How many times have you made that plain, to me, and to a lot of people?" Then Dance suddenly got up and walked to the window and stood looking down at the dark street. "We're talking like we always talked, old man, as if you were the bull of the woods and I was some damned skunk you'd come across." He turned back and sat down again. "Right now I want to get all I can for all the hurt you've caused me. But I can't do that, can

I? I've got to forget it like it never happened. I guess there's no getting even, starting from scratch. Old man, I want one thing settled here: never again do I want to lift a hand or a weapon against a Slate, and I want the same to hold true for me. It's got to be all over."

Christian Slate considered this with his head tipped forward; he spoke without raising it. "All my life I've dominated man and beast, but in the end I'm bowing to a woman." He looked at Dance then. "My wife called me to her and told what I had to do. She made it plain that I would do this or she'd leave me. I love that woman, Dance. I've treated her badly, but I love her. Losing her now was something I couldn't stand. Kyle, Leed, shake hands with your brother-in-law."

"Aw," Leed said, "do I have to?"

"You do it!" the old man shouted.

The handclasp was brief, fulfilling the letter of the order and nothing more. Then the old man said, "It's done, and it hurt less than I thought. Now, we've got some business to tend to. Some family business."

"Pa," Leed said. "Butler wanted to come up."

"Go fetch him then," Christian Slate said.

He smoked a cigar while they waited for

Butler, and it wasn't long; he had been standing downstairs in the lobby. When the door was closed, Butler stood with his back to it.

Christian Slate said, "As soon as it's daylight, we're going to the fork in the road and start scouting out the brush. A man doesn't move without leaving some sign behind, especially when he's in a hurry to get out of the immediate vicinity. Does that meet with your approval, Butler?"

"I have nothing against it," Butler said. "A note signed by you brought me to the fork in the road." He took it from his pocket and handed it to Christian Slate, who examined it. "Care to say anything?"

The fact that he had been used made the old man furious, but he contained it well. "It's my signature, my writing, but I never wrote that. I'd kill my own son for bushwhacking a man." He threw the note on the floor as though it were trash and he couldn't wait to be rid of it. "The bullet was for you, Butler. That's plain enough."

"The other day you were ready to kill me to get your own way," Butler said.

"Yes," Slate said. "But that was the other day. You were right, Butler. Riding on Roe Carlyle would have been stupid. But using my name to set a trap is a lot more stupid, as someone will find out."

"The man responsible won't be killed on the spot or hung," Butler said.

"He'll be turned over to you," Dance said.

The Slates opened their mouths to protest, then the old man let his close. "Dance speaks for all of us, sheriff. You have our word."

"That's good enough for me," Butler said. "Let's look at this from a practical side for a minute. Who's going to benefit by my being dead?" He shrugged. "My wife would get my insurance. You wouldn't have to worry about me stopping you from having your own bullheaded way, but I see no other advantage to my being dead."

"Someone wants the Slates to fight," Shaw Dance said. "Roe Carlyle? I don't know. It seems stupid to call the Slate wrath down, but he was sure asking for it in town the other night."

"Butler, if you were dead, who'd enforce the rules?" Christian Slate asked. "I've seen factions fight, and they can only do so when the law is weak or nonexistent."

"If I'm killed," Butler said, "someone is ready to take my place. What would a war mean here, Slate? Open conflict. A divided town. Both sides weakened eventually or destroyed. The only thing that would remain would be the land. The people can be replaced."

"By railroad people?" Kyle asked. His father looked at him a moment, then frowned.

"Butler, would that railroad fella go that far?"

"I don't know. It's something we'll have to look into."

Westbrook Arnold, who had had a lot of experience dealing with bunglers, did not express his anger by tone or appearance, but it was there and Roe Carlyle knew it. He sat in Carlyle's office and smoked a cigar while Carlyle walked up and down the room.

"When I suggested that you get the job done," Arnold said, "I didn't think you meant to do it yourself."

"I couldn't trust anyone with it," Carlyle said flatly. "You know and I know and that's enough."

"And the woman doctor suspects," Arnold said softly. "When one of your men got hurt, she came here to your office and pounded on the door for five minutes. It will be hard to convince her that you were asleep as you claim."

"Why didn't you tell me that sooner?"

Carlyle said quickly.

"Well, I was afraid you'd lose your head and shoot her." He rolled the cigar to one corner of his mouth and got up. "I suggest that you take things calmly for awhile. Naturally, I don't want you to contact me further; I'll get in touch with you, if need be."

"Are you backing out?"

"Hardly," Arnold said. "Consider it a stategic withdrawal until more secure plans can be formulated. But I want you to get Butler. Get him out of the way and move your men into town. See that they're armed. Cut off their source of supply and they'll come to their knees damned quick." He smiled thinly. "And a man is always more susceptible to a deal when he's on his knees."

"What about Dance and Bucher? Will the town be closed to them too?"

"It's closed to everyone not on our side," Arnold said. He pointed his finger at Carlyle. "Don't miss Butler again."

Carlyle remained alone for many minutes, thinking this over. He opened the drawer of his desk and from beneath a file of papers, took out the .38 Smith & Wesson. It would be foolish for him to keep the pistol now, so he went outside and stood for a moment, wondering where he could hide it. Then he thought of a place and tossed it onto the steeply pitched roof. The gun slid down, caught in the deep eave and hung there, completely hidden.

The paymaster had a pistol in his office and Carlyle went inside and down the hall. His key fit every door in the building, so he let himself in and without lighting a lamp, rummaged through the littered desk drawer until he found it — a .44 Merwin-Hulbert short-barreled pocket gun.

He locked the door and left the building and walked toward town, but went to Jane Meer's house. Carlyle was surprised to find lamps lighted and the front door opened, but, as he stepped onto the porch, he understood why.

Shaw Dance and Leed Slate were there, and Cove Butler came out with Jane Meer. Dance and Leed Slate carried a litter bearing Dance's wife; Carlyle stepped aside so they could pass through the door.

Jane Meer gave Butler several bottles of medicine. "The instructions are plainly marked on the labels. Tell your wife to call me at any time if she needs me."

"I will. And thank you," Butler said. As he stepped out, he glanced at Carlyle. "Up a little late, aren't you, Roe?"

"I couldn't sleep. A near tragedy, wasn't it?"

"Nearer than you think," Butler said evenly. "Roe, if she'd died, Shaw Dance and the Slates would have taken this town apart board by board until they found their man." He brushed past Roe Carlyle and followed the litter bearers down the hill.

Jane Meer said, "Come on in, Roe. Close the door."

She went into the kitchen and poured some coffee, waving her invitation for him to sit down. He said, "You're a wonderful person, Jane. I mean, it takes a big person to put aside their feelings. You being in love with Dance, yet saving his wife the way —"

"I'm not in love with Dance," she said. "I never was. Awhile there, I thought I wanted him because he could get for me exactly what I wanted — what I couldn't get for myself. But he can't. He's changed. She won him over to the Slate side."

Roe Carlyle frowned. "What did you want, Jane?"

"The town at my knees," she said. "I want them on their knees saying how wrong they were and how sorry they are and I want them to keep on saying it."

"Suppose," he said, "someone else could offer you that."

She looked at him. "You, Roe? I don't know. Could you?"

He shrugged. "Suppose we wait and see."

"You're playing a dangerous game, Roe. Of course you know that. I know you weren't in your office when you said you were. No, I didn't tell Butler about it, if that's what's worrying you."

"Why didn't you?"

She sat down and folded her hands. "I want you to remember something, Roe. Shaw Dance is a more dangerous man than the Slates could ever be, and I'll tell you why. Shaw Dance really has nothing to lose. If you destroyed this town, Roe, Dance wouldn't care. He'd just go back up that mountain and dig in his mine, or cut timber with Max Bucher. He doesn't need the town or you or anything. There is a line, a wall to which you could pin the Slates' back, but not Shaw Dance's. You remember that, Roe. He's got the mountain."

"It can be taken away from him," Carlyle said. "It would please me to do something the Slates could never do, to take that damned rock pile away from Dance." He bent forward and patted her hand. "I may offer you that as frosting on the cake."

"I like frosting," she said.

He took out his watch and looked at it.

"Well, I've been up most of the night. I'm going home and go to bed." He drank the rest of his coffee and got up. "No one in this town gives a damn for Roe Carlyle. He's just a man in a suit who runs the mine. I've been here six years and not one man has offered to buy me a drink. Even that fat German, Bucher, hates me. Why? What did I ever do to him? Or to any of them. Arnold, the railroad man, treats me with respect, but I can see the truth in his eyes; he regards me as a fool, someone he can use and drop when he no longer needs me." Carlyle smiled. "He's got a surprise coming. I'm going to get him his damned railroad, but not the way he thinks. Slate will sell, but he'll sell to me, for my price, and then Arnold will pay mine. I don't think a chair on the board is too much to ask, do you?"

"Don't reach too far, Roe. You may fall, and it's a long way down."

"Heights," he said, "have never frightened me. In fact, I find now that there are many things I'm not frightened of. I only thought I was. Goodnight, Jane."

He left the house, drawing his coat tighter against the predawn chill. A wind blew gently, bringing with it the first icy fingers of winter, and Roe Carlyle supposed that the first snow was falling around Dance's cabin.

The town was asleep, the main street dark except for lights in the hotel, and he walked over to Cove Butler's house. The gate opened noiselessly to his hand and he made his way around to the side where lamplight oozed through a partially shaded window. He could not get close to see clearly inside, for some thick bushes grew there and held him away. Yet he could see a part of a bed and knew that it was the sick room where Noreen Dance rested. Mrs. Butler came in with a tray and a teapot, then a man passed in front of the window, blocking out most of Carlyle's view. He could not see the man's face, but he knew it was Butler for the man wore his pistol butt forward on the hip and he had on gray striped trousers; Carlyle had seen Butler wear those trousers before.

Pushing down his nervousness, Carlyle took the .44 from his pocket and cocked it. Butler had his back to the window, and he stood near it, no more than three or four feet away. Carlyle sighted carefully and squeezed the trigger. The recoil, the blast, the shattering glass and Mrs. Butler's scream shocked him into action, and he dashed toward the fence, vaulted over it, and ran down the dark street.

He ran until he could hear nothing, then he stopped to get his wind and to ponder the enormity of the thing he had done. He was more proud of himself than frightened, like a boy who builds a bonfire and burns the whole town down.

Returning to the mine without being seen was not difficult, and he went back into the paymaster's office and put the gun back in the drawer, beneath the rubble there where it hadn't been disturbed for years and probably wouldn't be.

There was a couch in the room adjoining his office, and Carlyle stretched out on it and loosened his tie.

He was very tired.

The shot, the falling glass, and the scream all pushed together, shocked Cove Butler so badly that he dropped the coffee pot and splattered it over the kitchen floor. Then he reached across his body as he ran, drew his gun, and charged into the back bedroom.

His wife was sagged against the wall, both hands pressed over her mouth. Kyle Slate lay on the floor, kicking, gagging, his eyes rolling wildly. His body was bent into a backward arc, then he stopped moving and lay still.

Butler said, "Get your shawl! Go to the hotel for Dance and the old man! Hurry!"

Noreen, he saw, had mercifully fainted; he gave her none of his attention. He heard the front door slam as his wife fled the house, and he bent to examine Kyle. The bullet had taken him in the back, breaking his spine. Under any circumstance it would have been fatal, and Butler knew he had lived only a moment after the shot had been fired.

Butler dragged Kyle from the room and laid him in the hall, then covered him with a blanket. He got some water and a cloth and cleaned the blood from the floor, then Dance came in, and a moment later, Christian Slate and his remaining son.

The old man brushed past Butler and with the muzzle of his rifle he flicked the blanket away from Kyle. "Why?" he asked.

"Again the bullet was meant for me," Butler said. "He wears his gun the same way I do, butt forward." He went into the bedroom and pointed to the shade. "Down that far, anyone looking in couldn't see all of him; he was standing close to the window."

Butler's wife came in, her manner surprisingly composed; she made Noreen take a pill and a drink of water. Then she looked

189

at her husband. "Cove, go in the parlor. Please."

"I'm sorry," he said and ushered them out.

Christian Slate paused in the hall and glanced down at his dead son, and Dance covered him again with the blanket. They went into Butler's parlor and the old man stood there, his rifle cradled in the crook of his arm.

"The killer's in town," Dance said. "Leed, you come with me. Butler, you and the old man take the hotel."

"The railroad man?" Butler said, raising an eyebrow.

"He made me a halfway proposition once, didn't he? Make sure he wasn't out of his room when that shot was fired."

"Wait!" Christian Slate said. He looked at Butler. "The killer fired because he thought it was you. Right now he doesn't know he made a mistake."

"So?" Dance said.

"Let him go on thinking he got his man."

Butler's wife came into the parlor in time to hear that; she put her arm around Cove Butler and wiped a tear from her eyes. "What are you going to do, Mr. Slate?"

"I'm going to take my boy home, like a thief in the night, ma'am. I'm going to bury him with no words over him, and no marker over his head." He lifted the muzzle of the rifle. "And I'm taking you along, Butler, the easy way or the hard way. Then I'm going to flush me out a backshooting skunk."

"The word'll get out that I'm alive," Butler said. "Old man, it won't work."

"It'll work," Slate said. "I got an empire, and I rule it. No word will ever come from my place that you're alive. Butler, give me your word to stay at my house, as my guest, and there'll be no guard on you."

"And if I don't?"

"You'll live awhile with a gun always pointed at you."

Butler frowned and thought about this. Then he said, "I don't want my wife alone here now."

"In a week, ten days," Slate said, "she can leave, as soon as my girl's fit to be brought home. Take the stage north. Get off there. I'll have a buggy and a man waiting to fetch you to my place. I don't ask a man to live without his wife."

"Dance," Butler said, "I want no lynching now."

"What's he got to say about it?" Leed asked.

"Show him the badge," Butler said.

Shaw Dance exposed it, and Leed blew out an exasperated breath. "That's the last straw; a deputy in the family."

"We've got to move," Christian Slate said. "Be daylight in another hour."

"Wait a minute," Butler said. "We're making a big mistake. Don't I get a funeral? It's going to look damned funny —"

"He's right," Dance said. "I'll stay and take care of the arrangements; everyone knows that Butler and I were close friends. You take Kyle home. I'll get a casket from Londecker's and fill it with dirt and have it sealed come daylight. Cove, you go on with the old man."

"All right," Butler said. "I'll throw a few clothes in a bag."

"Leed," the old man said, "you go fetch my buggy. And do it quietly." He sat there and stared at the pattern in the rug. "Why is it I never have the time to shed a tear for anything? My paw was taken by Indians, and there wasn't time then. Two brothers were killed raiding a rustler's nest. No time then either." He looked at Shaw Dance. "Go to your wife, boy. She'll be wanting you."

Dance hesitated, then left the parlor and went into the bedroom. The lamp was low and he saw that Noreen was awake, but lethargic from the sleeping pill. He sat on the edge of the bed and bent and kissed her.

"You've been away for a long time," she

said. "It seems like we started for town a long time ago." Then she frowned. "Kyle! Someone killed Kyle!"

He put his hand gently over her mouth to hush her. "Now you've got to listen to me. Can you understand me?" She nodded and he took his hand away. "Yes, he's dead, but we don't want anyone to know it. Your father and Leed are taking him home. Cove Butler's going with them and everyone, including the killer, is going to think Butler's dead. I'm going to have to leave you for awhile, maybe a whole day. Mrs. Butler will be here with you. And you have nothing to be afraid of."

"Shaw, do you know what I thought when the bullet hit me?" She raised her hands to his face. "I thought I was going to die before I ever told you how much I loved you."

"You're not going to do anything but get well," he said, smiling. "And then we have a lot of things to say to each other."

Mrs. Butler opened the door slowly and looked in. "They're ready, Shaw."

10

Cove Butler's funeral, like all good funerals, was a properly solemn affair with many people attending to see how the widow was taking it. Shaw Dance made all the arrangements, and the minister made a fine speech about the qualities of the deceased and the casket was duly lowered into the ground and covered.

Afterward, with the widow safely home, Dance went to the bank to close out Butler's affairs; failure to take care of these small details would arouse suspicion, not from the man on the street, but from the one man who had pulled the trigger. The banker agreed to act as trustee and offer the house for sale when Mrs. Butler wrote him to do so. Dance spent several hours with the banker, then went across the street to Hanley's for a free lunch and a glass of beer.

Roe Carlyle was there, at his table, drinking alone; it struck Dance that this was pretty much the story of this man's life, doing everything alone, even the pleasureable things. After Dance ordered his beer, Carlyle left his table and came to the bar. A half dozen men stood there; they turned their heads, glanced his way, then went back to their own business.

"A sad thing," Carlyle said. "Butler was a good man. One of the best. Never met a fairer peace officer, or one who could handle his job better."

"He'll be missed," Dance said. "A hell of

a way to go out, shot in the back. I'll bet the bastard that did it is looking at himself now and wondering how a brave man like that can go on living."

"They're the dangerous kind," Carlyle said, "the ones who shoot you in the back. You've been lucky, Dance. You've never run up against a man like that." He sighed and motioned for Hanley to come and refill his glass. "We'll have to start looking for somone to take Butler's place. Can't be without the law."

Dance thought that now he ought to show Carlyle the badge, but a hand of caution held him back. "Never be in a hurry when you're picking a lawman, Roe."

Carlyle lifted his drink. "How's your wife?"

"Recovering. We'll take her home in a week or so. Mrs. Butler said she'd stay until then."

"Is she leaving?"

"What's to keep her here? Her folks are in San Francisco, or some place near there." He helped himself to the free lunch, then looked at Roe Carlyle. "This Saturday night, I suppose you'll pay again instead of waiting until next week."

"Naturally. Why should I adjust my schedule to Christian Slate's. If his men want to

195

come to town, it's their own risk." He chuckled. "As a matter of fact, it's about time Slate changed a few of his ways. Let him keep his men out of town for awhile. You tell him that."

"Tell him yourself," Dance said. "But be ready to high-tail it when you do."

"I think I'll let him find it out the hard way," Carlyle said. "That goes for you too, Dance. When you finish that beer, ride out and don't come back."

Dance stared blankly at Carlyle, too dumbfounded to move. Then he started to turn toward the man and stopped abruptly when someone behind him broke a bottle across the edge of the bar and said, "I'll bet I could cut your neck half in two with this thing, mister."

"Dance isn't going to give us any trouble, Harry," Carlyle said. "Do you see how it is, Shaw? Your woman's a Slate, so that lumps you in with them. When she's ready to move, you can come back for her; I'll see that you get an escort in and out of town. If you try to come back otherwise, you'll be hurt."

"You're out of your mind, Roe."

"No." Carlyle's voice was flat. "I'm tired of being caught in the middle. If you'd care to turn around, Shaw, I'll introduce you to the new Peace Commission. I appointed them as soon as Butler was killed."

"You move fast. Judge Heckett won't stand still for it."

"What can he do? Six strong men, always in pairs, always carrying a trusty shotgun under their arm." He smiled and spread his hands. "It's the new order, Shaw. Why fight it?" He reached out and tapped Dance on the chest with his finger. "You tell old man Slate how it is now. And I'm kind of hoping he tries to come into town. We'll have another big funeral."

"What does this really buy you, Roe? Besides a swelled head, I mean?"

"Power," Carlyle said. "The power to deal my way with people who have been loathe to deal with me in the past. Dance, do you think you're the only man who has a grudge against the world? Now I'd advise you to clear out of here. Harry, you and George go along with him. If he gives you any trouble, show the town how you deal with trouble-makers."

"Yes, sir, Mr. Carlyle."

Dance said, "Roe, you'll never live to be thirty-five."

He walked out and the two men with shotguns followed him. Hanley stood behind his bar, saying nothing, but watching

Carlyle. Finally he said, "You can't do that to people."

"Why not?"

"It ain't right," Hanley said.

"I'll decide that," Carlyle said. "Tell that around town."

He stood there until Dance left town, then he walked across the street to the hotel and went up the stairs. Westbrook Arnold was standing by the wash stand, shaving; he glanced at Carlyle in the mirror.

"Customarily we knock," Arnold said.

"We're doing away with the customary," Carlyle said. "Dance left town. I ran him out."

"You may think so," Arnold said. "Dance reminds me of a man I saw playing poker in Tascosa, Texas some years ago. The game was pretty one-sided, and finally this gentleman insisted that a new deck be produced. The heavy winner objected and got talky about it, claiming that he was being accused of cheating. The upshot was that he drew a pistol and upbraided the other for being a coward. And when the abused gentleman got up and left the game, the winner bragged about his ability to judge men. A few minutes later the man came back, only he had his pistol on his hip, and the tune rapidly changed. Dance, my friend, only left to get his pistol."

"A very funny story," Carlyle said petulantly. "I'm not afraid of Dance."

Arnold dried his face. "I suppose shooting a man in the back does call for some courage, although of a peculiar kind."

"Don't use that tone on me!"

Arnold threw the towel down and adjusted his collar and tie. "Carlyle, I may have to do business with you, but I don't have to like it or pretend that I do. You're a cheap opportunist, and you'd slit my throat in a minute if you thought you could gain by it. However, I have some advantage over you; I've dealt with your kind for years and I'm still around." He shrugged into his coat. "Now shall we discuss business?"

"When I'm ready," Carlyle said, "I may hurt you just for the fun of doing it." He took a cigar from his pocket and bit off the end. "Hanley doesn't like the idea of my blocking the Slate outfit from town. Not that he gives a damn about the Slates; it's the drop off in business he dislikes. Give me two weeks and I'll force every merchant in town to my side, and when I get their support, I can get them to apply pressure on the old man to sell that valley property."

"I'm ready to buy," Arnold said. "Count me in on the delegation that goes to see

Christian Slate."

Carlyle smiled. "I rather thought I'd buy it for you."

"I expected you to say that," Arnold said. "There's a limit to my authorization to pay."

"Oh, I don't expect to make a profit on it," Carlyle said. "My training is administrative. I was thinking of a position on the board."

"You're way out of your class, Roe," Arnold said. "It couldn't be swung."

"Let's say that it must be swung. You need this spur. It'll show a profit and rub out some of the red ink. Suppose you work on that little thing and I'll get your property; Slate can't live without this town, and the merchants can't live without Slate money." He got up. "We know where we stand?"

"I always did," Arnold said. "Carlyle, I have never considered you a very complicated man. Oh, I realize that you have the normal desires of a small man that have pulled you this way and that, but you still remain uncomplicated. I have merely selected the lowest common denominator of your basest desires, and judged from there. Now would you mind getting out of here?"

"If you expect me to give a damn about the town," Shaw Dance said, "you've made a bad guess." He stopped his pacing to face Christian Slate and Cove Butler. "Carlyle's a hog. He wants it all."

Cove Butler slumped in his chair before Slate's fire. He said, "Christian Slate's a hog; he wants it all too. Hell, we're all hogs in one way or another. It's just a question of whether or not we're all going to root in the same pen or not."

"You've got a blunt way of putting a thing," Christian Slate said. He turned to his son. "Leed, in the morning I want you to send a man to Virginia City and tell Morey about this trouble. Tell him to come on home now. I also want thirty more men put on the payroll in the next three weeks. And I don't give a damn if they can rope or not, as long as they can shoot."

"All right, pa."

Cove Butler said, "It takes two to make a fight. Carlyle's counting on that."

"Good, because I won't disappoint him." He looked at Shaw Dance. "Do you ride with me, son?"

"Yes," Dance said. "Carlyle's got to go, the hard way if it has to be."

"You swore to uphold the law," Butler said. "Shaw, I'm going to hold you to that."

"To me, that means getting Carlyle," Dance said. "Does anyone disagree?"

Leed was standing by the window; he said, "There's a rig coming toward the house. It's Bucher."

Dance said, "Better get out of sight, Cove. The few who know —"

"I agree," Butler said and left the room as Max Bucher dismounted and came onto the porch. Leed let him in and Bucher's expression was grave. He accepted the drink Christian Slate offered, then sat down.

"It's a sorry pass, the way things are," he said. "I saw your wife this afternoon, Shaw. She's feeling better and asking about when she can come home." He looked at Shaw Dance. "I'd get her out of that town as quick as I could, boy. Carlyle's moved into the hotel so he can hold audiences when he wants to."

"Is the railroad man still there?" Dance asked.

"Like a vulture on a perch," Bucher said. "After you get through carving each other up, he'll get what he wants. Funny thing about this whole thing is that Carlyle can't really win at all. I've heard talk that he means to make you sell the right of way to the railroad. I never thought that was reason enough to start a war. But I guess I've got it figured right now. Roe, he doesn't give a damn whether the railroad's built or not.

202

Not as long as he has his revenge against you, Shaw, and you, Christian. He's out to destroy you, not for money or position, but because he wants to get even for all the times you've looked through him or brushed him aside like he was some damned dog."

"That's not enough reason —" Christian Slate began, then stopped for a moment. Then he said, "Yes, I guess it's all the reason a man would need, and the best reason some men could have. You've touched the truth of the matter, Bucher. I do believe you have."

"His revenge may cost him his life," Dance pointed out.

"He's riding high and he isn't figuring on that. Well, I've had my say. Guess I'll be going back now. Thanks for the drink, Christian." He looked around the room. "First time I ever been in this house. A real nice place. My best to your wife."

Dance walked out with him and as Bucher got into the buggy, Dance said, "I suppose he wants my mountain too."

"He's always wanted that. He always claimed that when you and the Slates finished each other off, he'd ride up there and take it. Well, one thing good, you and the Slates have made peace."

"An uneasy peace," Dance qualified.

"Hell, most peace is," Bucher said and drove away.

Cove Butler had returned to the room by the time Dance came back. Butler said, "Sometimes Max really comes up with the truth. Christian, you could sell that valley right of way in the morning, and it wouldn't change Carlyle's mind a bit. Old man, you know who killed Kyle and shot Noreen. We all know it was Carlyle, but we couldn't prove it. I guess we won't have to, if it comes down to that. However, I want to tell you a few more truths. Your mule stubbornness about selling the right of way in the first place brought this on. You've had your way, but it cost you a son."

"Don't you think I know that!" Slate roared. Then he calmed himself. "Let's keep our voices down. My wife's a light sleeper."

"I'm not going to shout," Butler said. "I don't have to shout this. Carlyle's not much different than you, or even you, Shaw. For fifteen years you've made Dance's life one misery after another, old man. And Shaw, you've thought a lot about getting even with the Slates. Somehow, because of an innocent-eyed girl, it didn't come out that way. Maybe that pushed Carlyle over the edge, made him decide to act. But I want you to get it straight and to understand it,

204

that you all helped push him."

"Not directly," Shaw Dance said.

"Don't try to duck it," Butler said. "You know what I mean and you know that I'm right. You're the leader of the clan, Christian. Whether I like it or not, I've thrown my lot in with yours. What are we going to do about Carlyle?"

"Wait a few weeks," Slate said softly. "And when I can put a hundred and fifty armed men at my back, I'm going to ride him into a grave." He smiled. "Morey will be back. We'll be together again."

"He won't come back," Cove Butler said. "He's been away long enough now to have found enough troubles of his own and yours won't seem very important to him. He may send you some men, but he won't come back."

"I know my son!" Christian Slate roared.

"If that's any more than a hollow brag," Butler said, "then you know what I said is the truth. There's only two of you left, old man."

11

On Wednesday, Shaw Dance drove to town in a buggy to bring his wife home, and he was met at the end of the street by four of

Roe Carlyle's Peace Commission; they escorted Dance to Cove Butler's house and waited outside while Dance went inside to get his wife.

Butler's wife had Noreen's things ready; she only had a small canvas bag filled with the things Mrs. Butler had given her.

"Tell Cove that I'm taking the morning stage," she said quickly. "I'll wait in Virginia City for him."

"All right," Dance said. He picked his wife up in his arms and carried her outside and put her in the buggy and wrapped a blanket around her. The air was cold, and each morning the ice on the water buckets was thicker. Before he got in the rig, Dance turned to Butler's wife. "I don't know how to repay you —"

"Never mind the talk," one of the men said. "You've got what you came for. Mr. Carlyle doesn't owe you any more than that."

"Go, Shaw," Mrs. Butler said.

Dance got in the rig and lifted the reins, and the four men flanked him as he drove down the street and turned onto the main drag. As he drew near Hanley's, Hanley came out as though he meant to speak to Dance, but one of the men veered off and rode toward the saloon and Hanley went back inside.

"Just keep going," one said, and Dance kept a check on his temper. At the end of the street, the man said, "Hold up a minute."

Dance hauled the team to a standstill, then Roe Carlyle drove alongside in his buggy. He tipped his hat politely to Noreen, then glanced at Shaw Dance and smiled.

"I thought you might want to say goodbye to the town, Shaw."

"Why should I? I'll be back."

"Well, I rather expected that you would, so I've reserved a place for you in the cemetery. I trust this talk doesn't alarm you, Mrs. Dance. It's all up to your husband." He pulled up his coat collar. "Winter's just around the corner. I noticed some snow on your mountain. However, in the spring, when it melts, I expect it will be melting on *my* mountain."

Dance said, "You're having a good time, aren't you, Roe?"

"A delightful time."

"The railroad man too?"

Carlyle shrugged. "He's beginning to bore me. I may have to shoot him."

"He may not turn his back on you," Dance said evenly.

Carlyle struck him across the face with his

buggy whip and said, "Careful with your tongue, Shaw. I won't tell you that again!"

"Let's go home and let him have the town," Noreen said.

Carlyle laughed. "A sensible girl." He clucked to his team, turned about and drove on down the street. Dance waited a moment, then drove on, taking the mountain road. When he passed Bucher's place, he waved, and before he pulled out of sight, the German had saddled a horse and was riding out after the buggy. He caught up with Dance as they hit the bad stretch of road and followed him all the way to Dance's place.

Then Bucher dismounted and said, "I'll take care of the horses. You take Noreen in and light a fire."

Dance carried his wife inside and then built up the fire.

"Home is a wonderful place," Noreen said. She was a bit unsteady on her feet but she insisted on moving around, touching the table and her sink. Bucher came in, flogging his hands together and blowing on them. He scraped snow off his boots, then backed up to the stove where a new fire began to push out heat.

"I've been watching the road every day," Bucher said. "It's a lonely mountain without you, Shaw." He tamped tobacco into his pipe and lit it. "What's the old man going to do?"

"Fight," Dance said. "The call's out now for men. In another ten days or two weeks, we'll be ready to ride."

"I suppose it's the only way, but I hate to see it," Bucher said. "A lot of people in town will be hurt. Buildings will get shot up. Seems unfair to make them pay for it."

"What's in town worth caring about? My father left it because he hated it so bad he couldn't stay any longer." He went outside and brought back the coffee pot full of water and set it on the stove. "Carlyle's the one I want. That's all I want, Bucher."

"No, that's not all you want," Bucher said softly. "I wish it was, Shaw. I wish it was because then it would end. But it's got to go as long as the poison's in you."

"What poison?"

"The poison that kept you at war with the Slates. And when you made your peace with them, it was the same poison you turned against Roe Carlyle."

"God, he's asked for it!"

"There will always be men who ask for it," Bucher said. "Shaw, after Carlyle's dead, who will it be then that you hate, that you must destroy?"

"No one! I'll be through!"

"What are you shouting for? You know it's not true."

"Max, don't stand there and aggravate me!"

"I'm trying to pump some straight talk into you," Bucher said. "Girl, am I right or not?"

"He's my husband," Noreen said. "Whatever he does —"

Bucher waved his hands. "Spare me that pitiful recital. All right, Shaw. Have it your way."

"I'm having it the way it's got to be," Dance said. He sat down at the table and studied his hands. "Max, I know what you want. You want me to forget all the hurt people have done me. Forgive all the meanness I've had at the hands of others. I guess you expect I should stay on my mountain and work my own affairs and leave Carlyle alone."

"That's exactly right," Bucher said. "Carlyle can only make a fight; that's all that's in the man. Stay away from town. Let him have it and it will dry up around him. He can't maintain his position forever."

"I'm not the waiting kind," Dance said. "That's all I care to say about it."

"Someday you'll change your mind,"

Bucher said. "I hope it ain't too late."

He had a cup of coffee then got on his horse and rode down the mountain. Dance decided that Noreen had been on her feet long enough and made her get into bed. He sat in a chair by her bed and didn't try to hide his troubled state of mind. The things Max Bucher said bothered him, kept pushing at him, trying to assert an influence on his decisions.

Finally he said, "Carlyle doesn't really give a damn about the railroad. It's me he wants. He wants to put me down." Then he made a cutting motion with his hand. "That fat old man's soft in the head. Few people in town have ever trusted him, or bothered to get to know him, yet he feels kindly toward them. He ought to have learned by now."

"What would you have him learn, Shaw?"

"That people deserve less than you give them." He bent forward and kissed her gently. "Try and get some sleep. Butler will be here tonight."

Leed Slate and Cove Butler arrived at Shaw Dance's place two hours after nightfall and stomped the snow off their boots before coming in. The snow was falling in a gentle blanket and they both backed up to the fire with their coffee.

Butler said, "It's good to get out of that damned house." He glanced at Leed and smiled. "No offense meant toward the Slate hospitality."

"How's the snow on the lower reaches?" Dance asked.

"Falling," Leed said. "But not bad. You want me to hitch up the buggy?"

"I'd appreciate it," Dance said. He got his coat and mittens and rifle and dropped some extra shells into the side pocket. "I ought to reach Virginia City by late tomorrow. Give me a day and a half to get back."

Leed went out and Dance put some food into an old flour sack. Butler finished his coffee and refilled the cup. "The old man's like a bear in a cage," Butler said. "I feel sorry for Carlyle when he's turned loose."

"Bucher says we ought to let Carlyle have the town."

"It's the right way to do it," Butler said. "He'd either give it up or come to us. Either way we'd have him and little harm done. But then, when a man doesn't care about those things —"

"Now don't you start in on me," Dance said.

Leed came back and then Dance kissed his wife and went out and got in the buggy. He drove on down the mountain and took the north road. He had many miles and a long night to travel, and he settled down to it with a determination to get it done, yet he felt a growing uneasiness and for a time believed that it was because he had left his wife so that he could take care of this errand. Then as the night wore on he began to understand that Bucher was more than half right; a man couldn't go on looking for something to hate, and he supposed that if a deal could be made with Carlyle to settle this man to man, he should make it and not turn the town into a battle ground.

Dance was part of an army assembling, and he didn't want to be a part of anything; he was a man who liked being alone, and he saw no reason to change his ways now. Maybe it would be best, when he got back, to face Christian Slate and tell him that he wanted out. He had his wife back and he had his work with Bucher on the mountain, and, if Carlyle came up the hill, he'd handle him. But until then he knew he would have been better out of it.

There was a question in his mind now about the wisdom of throwing in with the Slates; he felt uneasy among old enemies, as though he expected they really hadn't put any animosity aside, but held it in abeyance for some more opportune time. Or maybe it was because the Slate way wasn't his way, and he wasn't accustomed to doing anything anyone's way but his own.

Dance stopped at a small town, and at a ranch before reaching Virginia City. He went to the hotel and found Mrs. Butler there, and told her they would leave as soon as it got dark. Then he went to the barbershop, got a trim and a shave, and a hot bath. Afterward he slept in the stable and at nightfall he drove around behind the hotel and escorted her down the back stairs.

There would be a surprised clerk in the morning, and Dance supposed they'd always talk about that woman who disappeared into thin air.

At no time had he really pushed the horses, and he didn't push them on the way back, but he kept up a steady pace, eating away the miles. The snowing had stopped and the night turned bitterly cold, and, although Dance had plenty of blankets, Clara Butler's teeth chattered.

At dawn he stopped and built a brush fire and made some coffee; this thawed them out somewhat. Dance said, "Being a lawman's wife is tough."

"Shaw, life is tough for everyone. Somehow you've never understood that. Even Hanley who runs the saloon has his troubles when men fight in there and break the chairs and the mirror now and then. But no matter what is broken, we have to pick up the pieces and go on."

Dance kicked the fire out. "What am I supposed to do, Clara?"

"You know. Break away from the Slates. You and Cove don't need them. Not now or ever." She put her hand on his arm. "You'll have to arrest Roe Carlyle. If you don't, there won't be any law except what Christian Slate makes."

"I guess that's about the truth of it," Shaw Dance said and helped her back into the buggy. As he started to drive on, he said, "You'll stay at my place. Cove can come there."

She smiled quickly. "Thank you, Shaw. I always knew you'd do the right thing."

He timed his return exactly, and made the frightening drive up the snow-packed mountain road in the dark, trusting more to the team than his vision. When he pulled into the yard, the cabin door opened and Leed stuck his head out. Dance said, "It's all right," and then Butler dashed out and lifted his wife down and kissed her.

"I'll take care of the horses," Leed said and Dance went on in the cabin and for a moment he couldn't decide what he wanted more, to put his arms around Noreen, or his cold hands around a cup of hot coffee. He settled for some of both.

Noreen was feeling better; Dance noticed that the full bloom of color had returned to her cheeks and although it would be a month or more before she could use her arm, she handled herself nicely at the stove.

"I've got some things I can heat quickly," she said. Clara Butler started to protest, but Noreen would not have it. "Now I know you've eaten cold for over a day. Please sit down."

"Arguing won't do any good," Shaw Dance said, smiling. He got out of his coat and heavy gear and hung them up. "Cove, I told your wife she could stay here." He looked at Butler and found the man standing there, not surprised, but attentive.

"This isn't the old man's plan," Butler said.

"I know. Maybe that danged badge is heavier than I thought. It's up to us, Cove, and there's really no two ways about it."

"You finally see it, huh?" He laughed softly. "I'm glad, because I couldn't have done it alone, Shaw. That may sound strange to you, to hear a lawman say that some things are just too much for him to handle, but I'm not that proud."

Leed came back in, pounding his hands together. He looked from one man to the other and immediately sensed the talk that had been going on.

Dance said, "Leed, tell your old man that Butler and I are out of this. We'll take care of Carlyle our own way."

"You know, I kind of thought you'd turn up your belly."

Butler said, "Son, don't make any hasty and wrong judgments."

"Who the devil is?" He looked at Dance. "Boy, blood sure tells, don't it? All right, I'll tell pa. But you'll never get a second chance."

"I don't need one," Dance said. "Maybe he'll have more sense than you and see that this has got to be done the law's way and not the Slate way." He waved his hand. "You'd better get going, son."

"It can't be too soon for me. This place has a stink to it."

He slammed out of the house and Cove Butler sighed. "Ah, the intolerance of youth."

Dance looked at him. "Who ever said it was confined to youth? Are we going to move tonight?"

"Yes," Butler said. "But I want to see Bucher first."

12

As Dance and Butler rode down the dark trail, Dance wished that Noreen had said something before he left; he wasn't sure what he had wanted to hear, but anything would have been better than her understanding silence. Butler, who rode behind Dance, said, "I never get used to it. Someday I'll quit and then she won't have to hold back every time I leave her to do my work."

"You read minds, Cove? Watch it here! The trail's narrow and there's a four hundred foot drop off." He eased the horse past the spot and did not speak until Butler pulled clear. "I don't like your job."

"No man likes it, unless he's got a killer instinct."

They found Bucher's cabin dark and first thought that he had gone on into town, but as they approached the place, a lamp went on and Bucher yelled, "Who's there?"

"Friends," Dance said and dismounted. He and Butler went in and Bucher closed the door. He wore only his underwear and quickly put on his pants. "You went to bed early tonight, Max," Dance said.

"I was tired. Don't you ever get tired?" Then Butler registered on him and he staggered back a step and said, "Good God! I stood at your graveside!"

"Pour yourself a drink, Max," Butler said. He explained what had happened. Then he sat down. "We've got some work to do tonight, if you'll help us."

"I'll do what I can," Bucher said.

"Carlyle has the town patrolled by his toughs," Butler said. "We've got to get into the town without being seen and get Carlyle. I think the best way to do it is in the back of your wagon, hidden under some empty boxes."

"I could make up an excuse for being in town," Bucher said. He looked from one to the other. "Where are the Slates?"

"We're alone," Dance said.

The fat man seemed pleased. "Good. It's the way it should be. I'll get my wagon hitched right away."

"Bucher, you just dump us in a dark alley and get out," Butler said. "You understand that?"

"All right," Bucher said. "I'm not much of a fighter anyway."

After Bucher went out, Dance said, "If Carlyle's as surprised to see you alive as Bucher was, it will weigh a lot in our favor."

"I'm counting on that," Butler said. "Carlyle's the only one I want tonight. With him a prisoner, the rest of the opposition will collapse."

"Where'll we hold him?"

"In jail," Butler said. "It's my jail. I had it built." He poured another short drink from Bucher's bottle, then went outside to wait. Dance followed him and they walked to the shed where Bucher kept his wagons and he worked in lantern light, making his final hitch. They helped Bucher load some large wooden boxes, then they got into the wagon and crawled out of sight.

Bucher got in and started to drive away, then he stopped by the cabin door. "Forgot to turn out the lamp," he said and went into the place. Then he climbed back onto the wagon and drove on to town. For Dance and Butler it was a cold, jarring ride and Bucher seemed to be in no particular hurry about getting there.

When they reached the end of the main street, wheel ruts, frozen into hard ridges, made the wagon bounce and slither about. Then Bucher drew up and a man spoke. "Oh, it's you. What are you doin' in this time of night?"

"I need some supplies," Bucher said. "With winter here, the men eat more."

"What's in the back of the wagon?"

"Empty boxes," Bucher said. "Take a look if you want."

"Thanks, I will," the man said. He came around and climbed into the wagon and began to shift boxes. Another man, standing near the head of Bucher's team, said something, but it was lost on Dance and Butler.

The man stirred the box under which Dance crouched, but he must have lifted the one that covered Butler, for he gave a cry of surprise, then Butler's .44 split the quiet of the street. Dance threw his box aside in time to see the man tumble out of the wagon, then someone fired a shotgun and he whirled, expecting to fight it out with the second man.

Bucher was standing up in the seat and peering down; he still held the shotgun with which he had killed his man. Butler said, "To the jail! Run that team, Max!"

He came out of his trance and lashed the team into motion, and, as they tore past the hotel, another of Carlyle's men appeared, and Shaw Dance put a rifle bullet into him in passing.

The man went down, badly hurt, but he was moving across the porch, dragging himself along the last Dance saw of him. Bucher slid the wagon on the icy street and crashed sideways into the hitchrail; all jumped down and Butler hurriedly inserted his key into the jail door.

As they went in, a number of Carlyle's men were gathering; Butler closed and barred the door, and went to the window, breaking out the glass with his pistol barrel.

"Get a fire going in here," he said. "If I've got to hole up, I'd at least like to be warm. Bucher, you'll find water in the hall to the cell blocks. Coffee and pot should be in that cabinet in the far corner."

Carlyle made his appearance and he carried no weapon, but he had a dozen men with him — men Dance and Butler had never seen before. They stood on the other side of the street, undefined in the shadows.

Then Carlyle said, "Dance, I told you not to come back into town!"

"Keep out of sight," Dance said softly. "He doesn't know you're alive, Cove." He put his face close to the window. "Why don't you come in and get me, Roe? It's cost you three men already. You've got too much in the pot to back out now."

"Who's in there with you?"

Bucher, fixing the fire, left his job and came to the window. "I'm in here. Me! Max Bucher! And I killed one of 'em myself."

"You fat little man, you made your big mistake tonight."

"The hell I did," Bucher said. Before Dance or Butler could stop him, Bucher

222

leveled his shotgun and fired the remaining barrel in Carlyle's general vicinity.

Immediately there was an answering burst of fire, but Dance had pulled Bucher to safety. The open door of the stove cast a red firelight onto the front wall, and Bucher shook his head.

"Sorry, but I just had to tell him."

"It's all right, Max," Butler said. He looked at Dance. "I can't really say that this is turning out the way I hoped it would."

"Is there another way in or out of here?"

"There's a back door, but it leads into the cell block and is iron-barred." Bucher finished stuffing wood into the stove and closed the door, and the only light that came from it was through the draft check door, like three red eyes in a child's pumpkin lantern. He came over and broke open his shotgun and refreshed the chambers.

Butler said, "You got that when you went into the cabin?"

Max Bucher shrugged. "I thought it would come in handy."

"So now you've got yourself in trouble," Dance said. "Max, you could have gone on home and no one would have know the difference. We told you —"

"I know what you told me," Bucher cut in. "We're partners, Shaw. And it goes deeper than that. I like to practice what I preach."

From across the street, Roe Carlyle said, "Dance? You're in a tough spot. How long do you think you can hold out without something to eat?"

"Long enough for you to get tired of this," Dance said. "You never did have much patience, Roe, and when you lose it, you make foolish mistakes. You want to rush me? I can hold you off with my rifle. And Bucher's got his shotgun and plenty of shells."

"I may not have to wait," Carlyle said. "I've got some new men. Came in a few days ago on the stage."

"I see you have some help," Dance said.

"One of them knows you," Carlyle said. "He wants to talk to you."

"I can hear him fine, if he has anything to say."

"No, he wants to come in. Alone. No gun. You're not scared of an unarmed man, are you?"

"Tell him to come over," Dance said. "We can handle him if he tries anything."

"There won't be any funny business," Carlyle said. "He's got something important for you to hear."

Dance looked at Butler. "You want to stand in the back hall, out of sight?"

224

"Yes, and I'll be covering you all the time," Butler said. He left his place by the window as a man came slowly across the dark street. He held his hands well away from his body and as he came onto the walk, Bucher unbarred the door and stepped back.

Shaw Dance was well away from the door, standing near the stove and when the man stepped in, he kicked open the stove door so that the light fell on him.

Dance drew in his breath. "Pa?" he said softly. "Is that you, pa?"

"Yep." He was a gaunt man in his late fifties, dressed in an old sheepskin coat and a sweat-stained hat. "I'd appreciate cozyin' up a bit to that fire there."

Dance stepped away, but left the door open. "Where you been, pa?"

"Oroville, Sacramento, and some north." He took out a pipe and tamped tobacco into it. "Around, but I heard about your mountain, boy. Heard you killed men over it."

"Only the ones who try to take it away from me," Shaw Dance said. "You still go by the name of Dance?"

The old man seemed surprised. "Why should I change it?"

"You ran from here once, so I supposed you'd change your name. What are you doing here?"

"I heard the money was good and that you were in trouble." He struck a match by touching it against the hot stove, and in the brief flare the family resemblance was strong.

"You're on the wrong side," Shaw Dance said. "Carlyle's a killer."

"So are you," Jack Dance said. "In case you're wonderin', Carlyle knows who I am. He don't trust me none, but I argued with him and won. I suppose he figured that if I changed sides now, it wouldn't make much difference." He turned his head. "Ain't you got a lamp in here?"

"I can see you good enough," Shaw Dance said. "You'd better go back to your boss, pa."

The old man grunted softly. "Would you shoot me?"

"If I had to, I guess I would, pa."

"That's what I wanted to find out," Jack Dance said. "When I left here, I hated so bad that I was scared to stay, scared it would come out and I'd be sorry for it later. But I had to come back to see what it had made out of my son. Not much, I guess."

"You didn't have to live here," Shaw Dance said. "Don't tell me what I am."

"I don't have to. You know. Coming back wasn't hard at all because I've got no hard feelings against no one. This afternoon, I went into Reilly's store, where your ma was killed, and we talked and I enjoyed myself. There's no desire for revenge in me, boy. And I don't want to leave here while any remains in you. You go on this way and you'll destroy yourself."

"It's Carlyle I want."

"He's nothin'. He's holding a short candle and it's about to burn his fingers." He knocked out his pipe and returned it to his coat pocket. "What'll you do after you get Carlyle? Go up there on your mountain and kill the next man who comes up there? What's up there anyway? A little gold? Some timber? Or a shrine that Shaw Dance built for himself? A shrine you know ain't real, ain't worth a hill of beans, and to keep anyone from finding it out, you put it out of their reach, hold it up like some damned prize, and defend it so they'll think it's something when it ain't. Boy, it takes more man to come off that mountain and live down here than it does to go up there and keep them off." He turned to the door. "I guess you've had it long enough. When you was little I whipped you for being bad. Now you're grown, but I've still got to whip some sense into you. I'm going to get my rifle and horse and go up there on that mountain.

You've had it long enough; it's time for another Dance to take it over. And if you want it, bring your rifle and come and take it back."

"You don't mean that, pa?"

Jack Dance laughed. "When was there a time when I say a thing I didn't mean? You come. I'll be waiting."

"Why?"

"You know," the old man said. "That mountain's a pile of rock with no real value to you. Any value it has is what you've put on it because you've hated these people all these years and had to show them you were the big man on the big mountain. But it's all a lie, son. You've got to find that out the hard way. So you come, and, if it's really important, you won't have any trouble about putting me in your gunsight."

"And me? Could you shoot me, pa?"

"Any man ought to shoot a critter he knows is dangerous." He opened the door then and stepped out and Max Bucher closed it and slid the bolt in place.

Bucher said, "What are you going to do, Shaw?"

Cove Butler left his place behind the cell block door; he holstered his revolver. "I can see which lion's den you were whelped out of. He meant that, Shaw. Every last word."

"Yes," Dance said. "The old man never said anything he didn't mean." He rubbed a hand across his face and his beard stubble whispered in the silence. "Do we get Carlyle first, Cove? Or do I take care of my family business?"

"You're not really going up there, are you?" Butler asked.

"If I don't, what am I in this town?"

"A friend of mine," Bucher said. "A good friend."

"And of mine," Butler said. "Shaw, let him have the damned rock pile. You don't need it."

"Which do we do first?" Shaw Dance asked. "Carlyle, or my business?"

Cove Butler sighed. "Let's get Carlyle."

13

Dance went to the window and looked out, and, as near as he could tell, the street was vacant; Carlyle and his men had withdrawn. "Take a look at this, Cove," Dance said and stepped aside so Butler could see out. "What do you make of it?"

"I don't know," Butler said. "Let's get out of here. Bucher, we'll try to get out the back way, although I suppose the alley is covered. Give us a couple of minutes, then you open the front door. Watch yourself, and, if anyone takes a shot at you, duck back inside and bolt the door. You'll have to lock the rear door after us."

"Suppose he don't miss?" Bucher said, then shrugged his fat shoulders. "Well, I'm getting old anyway. Get going."

Dance went first and slid the bolt on the rear door. He said, "I'll make the first jump and draw the fire. If I get clear, you follow me. Try not to give yourself away, Cove."

Butler unlocked the gun rack and took down a shotgun. "They know Bucher was carrying one of these and they may think we're going out together." He took Dance by the arm. "We're after Carlyle, remember?"

"I remember," Dance said. "Butler, understand me. I don't want to go up there now. But I've got to do it. Either that, or throw away everything I've built up." He opened the door and stepped into the black maw of the alley. He could see nothing, and Butler ducked out and crowded up close. Butler gave him a gentle shove toward the far end, and pointed, and they moved along cautiously, careful not to trip over any of the litter. There was a buggy parked near the end, and both men stopped to consider this unexpected development.

Dance whispered, "I'll go on. If it's all right, I'll strike a match." He left Butler before the man could offer an opinion, and approached directly behind the rig, crouching low so as not to be seen. At the rear wheels he stopped, then in one jump reached the side of the rig and jammed the muzzle of his rifle against the driver's side.

Jane Meer gasped and choked off a cry before it passed her lips.

"What are you doing here?" Dance asked.

"Waiting for you."

He found a match and struck it against the iron wheel rim then fanned it out quickly; Butler came up and looked into the buggy. For a moment Jane Meer did not recognize him; it was that dark, then she gasped and put her hands over her mouth.

"My God, I thought you were dead!"

"Keep your voice down," Butler said. "Where's Carlyle and his bunch?" He brushed past Dance and took her by the arm. "Why are you here in this alley?"

"Waiting for Shaw," she said. "I thought that he might need a quick way out of town when he made a run for it." She tried to shake her arm free of Butler's grip. "Let go of me. What's the matter with you anyway?"

"I've got a suspicious nature," Butler said. "How did you know Dance was in the jail?"

"I heard the shooting."

"That wouldn't tell you where he was. Try again."

"We're wasting time," Dance said.

"I want to hear this," Butler said. "Tell me."

"Oh, I heard the yelling. Someone told me. What difference does it make?"

"A lot," Butler said. "Carlyle's not an ass; he'd have covered this alley at both ends right away and he wouldn't let you or anyone else park a buggy here."

"I came after they'd all gone," Jane said. "Butler, you're a fool. Shaw could be on his way out of town."

"Where would you take him?"

"To his place, of course. Once he's on that mountain, a thousand Carlyles couldn't get him off. Get in, Shaw. Let him stand here and argue with himself if he wants to."

Dance said, "Why do you want me to go to my place, Jane. I was figuring to light out in the other direction and not stop until I got to San Francisco."

"You can't do that!" she said quickly. "Shaw, would you give up exerything now? The mountain is yours and the town can be yours if you'll go up there now. What kind of a father has he been to you anyway. Don't let go now, Shaw. Hang on, for both of us;

we have to show people, Shaw. They are their rules, not ours."

Cove Butler said, "Heard enough, Shaw?"

"Yes," Dance said. "Where's Roe, Jane?"

"Why do you keep asking me that? I told you I didn't know."

"You know because Carlyle sent for you. How else could you know my dad's up there waiting for me?" He stepped back away from the rig. "You told me once that I sought revenge against people, while you sought it against society. That's really a horrible thing, Jane. It's worse than being crippled."

"We're running out of time," Butler said. "I'm going to ask you once more and this time you'd better answer me. Where's Carlyle?"

"On the mountain," she said. "He knows Shaw will go up there, and he knows he'll fight his own father because he's been too long this way to change. Roe doesn't care who wins, because he'll kill him anyway."

"Get out of the buggy," Butler said.

He waited while, wordless now, she got down from the rig. Then he turned to Dance. "All right," he said, pushing Dance into the buggy. Then he got in and lifted the reins. "In the dark, Carlyle will only see two people, and he expects one of them to be Jane Meer." He turned the rig onto the main street, and, as he passed in front of Hanley's, he saw Bucher standing there with his shotgun under his arm, as though he had the whole town buffaloed.

Butler wheeled near the curb and motioned for Bucher to come over. "Where's Carlyle's toughs?"

"Inside, bellied up to the bar," Bucher said. "They never said boo to me. Guess I wasn't important enough."

"Bucher, did you ever arrest a man?"

"Nope, can't say as I have." He smiled. "But I've got my shotgun and I'm not afraid to pull the trigger if I have to. So if you'd like those fellas in jail by the time you get back, consider it done."

"You'll have trouble," Dance said.

"I'll handle it," Bucher said. "Go on after Carlyle." He turned toward Hanley's swinging doors as Butler drove on toward the edge of town. They just passed the last of the buildings when a shotgun roared in Hanley's place.

"He's found his trouble," Dance said.

"He'll know what to do about it," Butler said. "I guess he's either dead now, or shown them what kind of a man he is. Either way, Bucher'll be happy about it."

They soon passed the dark saw camp; all

of Bucher's men were in bed and not at all concerned about Shaw Dance or Roe Carlyle or anything except the hard day's work ahead of them. The good section of road finally ended, and for safety's sake, Butler handed the reins to Shaw Dance and hunched down in the seat.

The night was starless, and the moonlight was blocked off by a layer of high clouds; a raw wind husked against the mountains and blew particles of snow into drifts.

Butler suddenly reached out and hauled on the reins, stopping the buggy. Below them, on the town road, a band of horsemen drummed along and the thunder of their passing lasted several minutes.

Shaw Dance said, "Slate and every man he could put in a saddle. He's going to be disappointed."

"Isn't that sad," Butler said, and Dance drove on.

With snow on the road, Dance drove very carefully, still the buggy slid several times and he was barely able to check it in time to keep it from going over a long drop. Each time Butler would sigh and swear softly under his breath and wait for the next close call.

When they neared the top, Dance stopped the buggy and got down. "You take it on in to the clearing," he said. "Pull right over to the shed and stay there." They could see Dance's cabin, and there was lamplight in one of the windows, but no sign of anyone moving about.

"Where do you think Carlyle is?" Butler asked.

"In the rocks." He motioned to a higher prominence off to the right. "It'll give him his best view of the house and yard. I always holed up there when an unwanted visitor used my road. Not knowing the land well, it'll be tough to do, but if you could work your way around behind the shed and —"

"I'll take care of it," Butler said. He took the reins. "Shaw, you wouldn't kill him, would you? He's your father."

"The problem is, would he kill me?" He fell silent for a moment. "If I was you, I'd make that dash to the shed a dead run. He never could shoot worth a hill of beans, but maybe he's improved since I last saw him."

"Shaw, what are you going to do?"

"Try to get to him and take that gun away from him before he hurts himself with it," Dance said, then gave the team a lick that sent them into a dead run. Butler bowled into the clearing and from the house a rifle opened up, but Butler didn't stop until he reached the shed.

As soon as Shaw Dance saw the muzzle flash, he sprinted toward the west edge of the clearing, meaning to skirt the house while his father's vision was marred by the muzzle flash. Butler, with great presence of mind, fired his revolver at the general vicinity of the house, hoping to lull Jack Dance into believing the son was holed up there.

Even Carlyle might be fooled by that move, Shaw Dance thought and worked his way back to one of the rear windows. There was no rear door to the place, just the back bedroom windows, and they were dark. When he looked in he could see a strip of light coming from beneath the door, so he guessed that Noreen and Clara Butler were shut in there to keep them out of the way.

Very softly he tapped on the window and both women pressed their faces against the glass. They saw him but they made no sound and then they quickly pulled away and Dance barely had time to duck down before the door flew open and the old man looked in to see if everything was all right.

Dance remained crouched down until Noreen tapped lightly on the glass with her fingernails; he raised up then and saw that the door was again closed. The window would not open, yet Dance had an idea that it was worth a try. Still, he couldn't communicate with either his wife or Butler's for fear his father would hear.

He resorted to sign language, and it was a trial and error, repeat and repeat affair. Yet he managed to convey what he wanted. He would go around to the front corner, and they would smash the window. This would bring the old man on the run and give Shaw Dance time to break through the door and cover the old man before he could fire a shot.

When he was sure they understood, he skirted the cabin, hesitated until he heard glass crash down, then raced for the porch. He hit the door fast and hard and the bolt splintered and he went into a tumbling roll into the room.

As he started to get up, Jack Dance said, "Hold it right there."

Shaw Dance looked around and found the old man standing in the far corner; he hadn't even taken a step toward the bedroom door. His rifle was pointed at Shaw Dance, and he said, "Shove that Winchester away from you, boy. Give it a good shove."

Dance skidded it across the room, then got up slowly. "Well, why don't you shoot me?"

"Will if I have to," Jack Dance said. "Who's out there with you? That fat man?"

"Cove Butler."

Dance frowned. "Ain't he supposed to be dead?"

"He's supposed to be, but he ain't," Shaw Dance said. "What are you going to do, pa?"

"Call Butler in here." He walked over to the lamp and turned it down, then stood in front of it so that his shadow covered the door. "Go on, call him."

Dance went to the door and started to open it. "Just a crack now," Jack Dance warned. "Give him a yell, then back away from the door."

After a hesitation, Shaw Dance said, "Come in! I got him!" He stepped back and waited and a moment later, Cove Butler ducked inside. When he saw the old man holding the rifle, he stopped short, then tossed his pistol on the floor.

"It's been a poor day anyway," Butler said. "All right, Mr. Dance, you call the tune, and I guess we'll do a jig to it."

"I'm going to give him the first move," the old man said, pointing his rifle at Shaw Dance. "You want to pick up that gun, then do it, and use it."

Shaw Dance flicked a glance at Cove Butler, then said, "I can't."

"What do you mean you can't? I took your

damned mountain away from you, didn't I?"

"The rifle's not loaded," Shaw Dance said. He smiled weakly at Butler. "On the way up, I took the shells out of it and dropped them alongside the road, one at a time. I guess I shouldn't have done that. I should have left it loaded to see whether or not I'd have used it." He looked at his father. "Enjoy your mountain, pa."

"What would I do with it?" the old man asked. Then he laughed.

This irritated Butler; he didn't see anything funny at all.

The old man stopped laughing and rapidly worked the lever of his rifle and no ammunition cascaded out of it. "I guess I didn't trust myself either," he said.

"You fired a shot when I drove in," Butler said.

"Fifteen feet over your head," Jack Dance said.

"Would it be asking too much," Butler said, "to release the women? You must have them locked up someplace."

"They're in the bedroom," the old man said. "The door ain't locked. Never was." He saw the surprise on his son's face. "She had to find out too, I guess, just what kind of a man she'd married."

Butler walked across the room and flung the door open; he did not appreciate any of this and his manner reflected it. Noreen and Clara Butler came out, but said nothing.

"Well," Butler said, "now that this family business is over, could we load our firearms and catch a killer?" He bent and swept up his pistol and jammed it deep into the holster. Then he turned the lamp up high and went to the door. "I'm going out. I want him to see me. Do I go alone?"

Shaw Dance and his father dipped into their pockets for cartridges and shoved them into the loading gates of their Winchesters, and Cove Butler smiled.

14

Because he was the law, Butler was the first out the door, and he went through fast and made it, but Jack Dance, shoving his son aside to be second, caught Roe Carlyle's first shot in the thigh and spun as he fell. Shaw Dance would have stopped, but his father shouted him on, and, as the two men sprinted across the yard, the old man dragged himself back into the cabin and one of the women closed the door.

As soon as they reached the shelter of the shed, Butler stopped. Dance came up and motioned in a circular manner and Butler nodded, then began to work his way back into the rocks while Dance waited. After a few minutes elapsed, Dance left the shed and ran across the yard.

He drew fire, and answered it on the run, not stopping. Carlyle shot once more, then Dance veered and headed for the jumble of rocks and gained their shelter before Carlyle could shoot again. Carefully he began to climb; he had a pretty good idea where Carlyle was holed up. The snow hampered him, made slippery going of it, and he had to keep himself under cover or draw Carlyle's fire again. Dance only hoped that he was keeping the man interested enough so he wouldn't notice Butler coming in from the other direction.

A movement caught Dance's eye, then a sound came to him from below, near the shed. He abandoned caution then and skidded and slid until he was in the pocket Carlyle had occupied. Butler came up and swore, and then Carlyle tore out of the yard in the buggy.

Dance shouldered his rifle, but Butler put out his hand and blocked the hammer's fall. "He'll never make it now," Butler said. "Go saddle two horses. I'll see how the old man is."

They hurriedly left their place in the rocks and Dance trotted toward the shed and worked fast. Butler returned as he was finishing. "He's swearing a blue streak, so I guess he's all right." He stepped into the saddle and followed Dance from the yard.

Before they traveled a half a mile, Shaw Dance pulled up and pointed to the wheel cuts through a snow bank where team and buggy had gone over the side. Butler struck a match and then the wind blew it out.

"You knew this?" Dance asked.

"Figured it," Butler said. "He was in a hurry, and Roe was never a man to let anyone else do anything, 'cause he always figured he could do it better. Instead of letting the horses pick their way, he drove them and missed the turn." He turned up the collar of his coat. "I'll go on into town and get the doctor for your old man. Better go on back and wait, Shaw."

Butler went on down the trail, and Dance remained for a few minutes. Carlyle was no doubt at the bottom and dead, and it would be spring before the snow thawed and delivered up the body; it was a long time away. In a way, Dance felt sorry for Carlyle, for in the man he saw traits of himself, and flaws in himself. He was like me, Dance thought. He couldn't accept himself for what he was.

Then he turned and rode back up to his cabin.

Jack Dance was in bed and Clara Butler had a good fire going and coffee making when he stepped inside and hung up his coat.

Noreen looked at him, and he said, "Cove's gone into town to fetch the doctor." His glance touched Clara Butler. "Carlyle missed a turn going down the mountain."

"A bad end," she said. "But then, he was a bad man, wasn't he?"

"No worse than any other," Shaw Dance said. "It just got the best of him, that's all." He stepped into the bedroom, but left the door open.

Jack Dance said, "I didn't last long, did I?"

"You're all right, pa." He pulled a chair around and sat down. "Is there any reason you can't stay on?"

"I stay where I'm wanted," he said. Noreen came in with a tray and some coffee.

While she poured, Shaw Dance said, "Pa's going to stay on."

"I heard," she said. "You'll have to add on."

"Well, maybe in the summer I'll —"

"In the spring," she said.

He shrugged. "Spring then." He took her hand and held it. "I've put it off too long now, so I'll say it. What started out bad has turned out good for me. I love you, Noreen."

"I'm glad," she said, smiling. "It'll make everything easier."

"What easier?"

"I think I'm carrying," she said and hurried out.

The old man laughed. "Well, don't look so stunned. Go on with her. Hell, I'll be all right here until the doc comes." He waved his hand. "And close the damned door on your way out."

Shaw Dance went back into the main room and walked over to his wife; he put his arms around her and kissed her and didn't care whether Clara Butler watched or not.

"I'll have to hire a crew and widen the road," he said. "People will be coming up here and it won't do to have them risk their lives on that wheelbarrow trail." He helped himself to the coffee and stood with his back to the heat. "I'll take you home to see your mother in a day or two. She'll want to know. Maybe when it's your time, you can go home for awhile and —"

"No, I'll stay here," she said.

Max Bucher came into the yard and Dance opened the door and he came in, blowing on his hands. He nodded politely to Clara Butler, accepted coffee, and then stood by the fire.

"Christian Slate's on his way," Bucher said.

"What happened in town? I heard a shotgun —"

"Yes," Bucher said sadly. "A man died. Too bad."

"What did the Slates do?"

"Rode up and down the street. There was nothing for them. They roughed up the railroad man a little, but I stopped it." He let Noreen take his coat. "And things here?"

"Settled," Shaw Dance. "Pa's staying on."

Bucher nodded; he could get the details later. "I met Butler. He told me it was all over. Well, there'll be others like Carlyle. It's life."

"I don't have to take them on," Dance said. "I want to widen the road to the top, Max. And I haven't been giving the time to our business like I should. I'll make that up to you, Max."

"It's all right," Bucher said. "I knew how it was. We'll likely get rich, but I guess it won't change much. I'll still be a fat man with gravy stains on my suit. And people will remember and talk about you. I guess you won't mind now though. When a man grows enough so that he don't need a mountain to make him tall, he's able to take anything in stride." He lit a smoke, then added. "What are you going to do when Christian Slate shows up?"

"Ask him in," Shaw Dance said. "What else?"

"That's right, what else?" He smiled. "Doc Meer is going to be wondering —"

"She doesn't have to," Dance said. "I'm sorry for her. Not because she lost, but because she can't give up. Maybe in time."

"Time does wonders," Bucher said. "We may even get a railroad, if we name the town Slateville. It's an idea of mine I've been toying with."

"We'll have to give it a try," Dance said. "Why don't you go in and keep pa company?"

"I'll do that," Bucher said, smiling. He sighed. "Bad day, good day; who can tell? Good for you and me, and bad for Roe. It's always that way."

After he closed the bedroom door, Clara Butler said, "I like that man." Then she smiled brightly. "I like you too, Shaw."

"I guess I like myself, finally," he said, and

looked at his wife, for she knew what he meant.

CPSIA information can be obtained at www.ICGtesting.com
Printed in the USA
LVOW041636210113

PP7345000005B/1/P